Into the Ruins

Issue 8
Winter 2018

Published March 2018 by Figuration Press
Portland, Oregon

Into the Ruins is a project and publication of Figuration Press,
a small publication house focused on alternate visions of the future
and alternate ways of understanding the world,
particularly in ecological contexts.

intotheruins.com

figurationpress.com

ISBN 13: 978-0-9978656-6-0
ISBN 10: 0-9978656-6-0

Editor's Note:
What feels like an eventful year ahead.

Comments and feedback always welcome at editor@intotheruins.com
Comments for authors will be forwarded.

Issue 8
Winter 2018

TABLE OF CONTENTS

PREAMBLE

THE PROBLEM WITH "COLLAPSE"

BY JOEL CARIS

CHANGE IS A SNEAK. It comes upon you slowly, in increments often unseen, the unnoticed ticks of a clock that pass minutes, hours, days. It is the accumulation of thought and consideration and experience, teased out over months and years. It is the way that an idea once unthinkable, or at least unpalatable, eventually becomes commonplace—becomes habit. It is who you are now, often so different from who you were then.

Of course, change is not always that. Sometimes it is dramatic and sudden. Sometimes it's a break, severing what you once knew for a different reality now dominant. But most change takes place day by day, under the cover of mundane routine, via processes that churn always in the background. It's the accumulation of the new and the sloughing off of the old. Much of the new, as it turns out, is just the same as the old; but enough over time is different to create long term change. That's how the world eventually looks different. That's how futures are made.

When does it happen? When does "The Collapse" occur? That's the question so often asked about the future facing us. We want to know when the break will happen —where on the timeline the shearing off will take place. And it's the wrong question. More often than not, "The Collapse" never occurs—it just suddenly is noticed one day. The world, we realize, has changed. We think back ten years, twenty, and marvel at the ways it is different now against then. We come to recognize all the things that, if seen in advance, would have been shocking then but are routine today.

"How did we get here?" we ask ourselves, each other. And the oft-imagined cliff, the dramatic moment when everything changed, is rarely the answer.

"Incrementally," someone says. "One step at a time."

‡‡

It's not that there aren't moments. There are so many moments. We could name them together, we could make our lists. 9/11. Hurricane Katrina. 2008. The election of Donald Trump. These are recent ones we can point to freely, easily, reeling off the tips of our tongues. They were moments of collective shock, of widespread realization that we had entered into new territory, that the world and its terms of engagement had changed. Not that no one predicted these events in advance; varying people did in every case, at varying levels of specificity. But the society, the culture at large, did not. And when these moments hit, we (or at least some) suffered collective breaks. We tried, and often failed, to understand—even when there were perfectly reasonable explanations. We panicked.

Of course, there are endless other moments. How many foreign entanglements have we wrapped ourselves in? How many dead end economic policies have we enacted? How many ecosystems have we destroyed in the name of progress? How many sustainable livelihoods have we outlawed? How many seemingly inexhaustible resources have we exhausted? How much clean water, fresh air, and fertile soil have we polluted and ruined and wasted?

Each of these is a step. Most of them go unnoticed, or noticed by only a few. Most of them are simply manifestations of business as usual, and are insisted to be necessities, inevitable—even though they are neither. None of them are cliffs or cleavings—at least, until one of them becomes the black swan that brings a chunk of the system down and changes the terms. That's when we suddenly notice the change, but not generally the cause. 9/11. Hurricane Katrina. 2008. Donald Trump. Here again, they roll off the tongue, but rarely the underlying issues and actions that created them in the first place. Those unspoken truths are too often obscured at all costs. They have to be, so that we may take the next step.

But these black swans are not system-destroyers. They are not "The Collapse." They are wrenches. They break some gears, shut down a process. But overall, the system continues. It grinds on, hobbled, but with most everyone working to restore its function. And so they do, returning it not to its former glory (so to speak) but to some reduced version of it. And then, exhausted, they look for the next step to take. And the timeline of history continues.

There is nothing new about a civilization collapsing. It's happened time and time again throughout history, and it so happens that it's currently happening to our civilization. It shouldn't be a surprise; all the signs are there for those who care to learn the history. Nor should it be a surprise that it takes awhile, takes centuries. That means that, while we are currently living through the collapse of our civilization, we almost certainly won't live to see the final shape of the ruins. There's still a very long path to travel to get there. Still, the section that we have the pleasure of traveling, already proving eventful, is sure to become more interesting yet.

That entire path—hundreds of years long—is "The Collapse." But it will be filled with myriad events, many of them significant, far more insignificant, and with long stretches of relative calm. That's how a civilization collapses, not all at once and in flames, but piece by piece, step by step, some of them large and some small. It's a process. It accumulates.

Again, that's not to say there aren't meaningful moments or even sudden endings. We all will have a sudden ending some day, and many of us may have one directly related to collapse: an act of war, a failure of critical infrastructure, dramatic political or social turmoil, the lashings out of a population with its back against the wall, an escape from one's harsh reality that turns unintentionally permanent. Or perhaps we perish in an earthquake, a storm, some natural calamity. These too are part of the fractal pattern of collapse, driven sometimes by our own stupidity and other times by the natural processes that serve both to keep us alive and to eventually kill us.

The key to these events, dramatic and shattering as they are for those caught in them, is that they are localized. They may be localized at a very small scale or at a large, regional one, but they do not consume the entire world and, even where they are localized, they do not impact everyone at an equally disastrous level. In addition to their localization, they are inevitably mitigated. From the individual level all the way to the global, humans and their institutions tend to work to mitigate the overall impact of these disruptions and to limit their ongoing fallout. They seek stability and a return to normal. They respond, provide care, assist, and rebuild. Granted, these palliative actions can be too limited in scope, suffer from corruption, take too long, and feature exploitation and profiteering, but the responses still occur.

All of this serves to check and contain the spread of disaster. The impact is still there and the overall system suffers, but it isn't destroyed. It continues on at some lower level of function, awaiting always the next disaster that will piece it still a bit more apart, inch it ever closer to the final floor.

This is how civilizations die.

It's with this understanding and viewpoint in mind that I evaluate the stories I publish here in *Into the Ruins*. This magazine has been referred to as post-apocalyptic, but it really is not that, as I don't believe in apocalypse and I actively shy away from stories depicting such futures. Nor is it dystopian, as I instead search out stories that depict the kind of complicated world we humans make for ourselves—good roiled with bad—rather than the endlessly bleak and stifling futures so often depicted in dystopian stories. No, the stories I look to publish are those that take place in the changed worlds we're most likely to get, in which the slow process of collapse is quite a bit farther down the road or long since finished and completed, depending on the story.

That means, of course, that the stories I look to publish depict futures that are different from today, sometimes dramatically so. That's nothing new to science fiction, of course; however, the particular sort of science fiction found in *Into the Ruins* suffers from a distinct disadvantage that the usual stars-and-spaceships or all-computers-all-the-time sort of science fiction doesn't: that is, that the future depicted is not the one most people think we're supposed to get. A story featuring space adventures and interstellar travel is rarely under any pressure to explain how humans managed to get their way to that future if the writer isn't interested in a long explanation of the backstory. It can go merrily along on the presumption that the audience will take this future in stride, understanding that *of course* we'll eventually be happily planet-hopping with nary a second thought as to it's cost or feasibility, never mind the fact that no human has been beyond low-earth orbit for well over forty years now. However, a story set in a future in which industrial civilization has collapsed—or is in the process of doing so—and the populace is struggling with dramatically lower standards of living, reduced energy and resources, and the consequences of climate change, ecological collapse, rising seas, drought and famine, and other such obvious repercussions to our current ways of life . . . well, that's a future that must be explained.

In some ways, there's nothing wrong with that. An explanation of how humanity got to an imagined future is often intriguing when handled right, and a good part of the point of *Into the Ruins* is to help broaden the public's understanding of the predicament we're in through the use of fiction. Tracing out the consequences of that predicament, then, is a worthy effort. However, there are a ton of great stories waiting to be told in realistic futures that are worse off for having to hold the reader's hand through an explanation of how we got there. Just as a rip-roaring tale of space adventure might be knocked off track by a long explanation of the evolution of space travel, so too might a rip-roaring tale of adventure in a future wracked by risen seas, mass migration, and the desertification of large swaths of the American landscape might be knocked off its rhythm by a segue into the evolution of climatological change and disruption due to the exploitation of fossil fuels.

Our task at hand, then, is to make visions of these sorts of futures common. It's to make them as obvious and unquestioned as those with intergalactic space travel. It's to rid ourselves of the need for shorthand, of the need to clarify to the reader that something went wrong. It is, admittedly, a big task. But it's getting easier.

‡‡

One of the tropes of deindustrial science fiction is the tendency of characters to reference the moment when things fell apart, to give it a name like "The Collapse" or something else short and catchy. You can find examples of this phenomenon in stories in this very issue of the magazine, not to mention in multiple back issues. As the steward of this project, coming across such a term in a story always sets me a little on edge, gets my back up. I mean no disrespect to the authors who do it, mind you, because I understand the urge; it's for the reasons stated above, the assumed expectations of the readers. But it sets me on edge anyway because it puts the scent of fast collapse into the story. It teases at a possible past apocalypse. And that's one of the biggest reasons I reject stories that otherwise feature quality writing and an interesting story set in a compelling future setting: because they portray the collapse too fast.

Getting this right is important to me. If we're to understand the future that's unfolding around us and have a chance to address it head on—making the world a bit better, even if the emphasis is on "a bit"—then we have to understand that the collapse of a civilization is not an overnight, apocalyptic event. *It's what's happening to us right now.* It's only in comprehending this that most of us might begin acting now, rather than waiting for an apocalyptic act to kick us into gear. And it's in understanding that *this right now* is what the process of decline looks like that we may come to truly grasp that the future is not likely to be one of betterment, but one of decline, fraught with great challenges and great tasks at hand.

One of the biggest goals of this publication is to drive home that point through fiction. I don't carry that goal in an effort to depress my fellow citizens or to rage against the world; I carry it due to my own optimism, even if that optimism is sometimes buried a bit deep under cynicism. I really do believe that, facing a hard future, we can take actions that make that future better for us, our descendants, and the many other creatures who call this planet home. These actions won't fully mitigate what we are destined to face, but they can help, and I believe that such action is worth it.

But there are two common beliefs that do an excellent job of diffusing the sense of need for such action: the belief that the future is one of inevitable betterment, and the belief that the future is one of inevitable apocalypse. If the former, no action is needed, as we are not facing challenging times. If the latter, no action is helpful, as we are facing destruction anyway. Both beliefs foster a willingness to continue living lives that we know are dead ends, clearly are destructive, and that tend to fail in providing happiness and fulfillment, anyway. Both beliefs sentence us to a worse future, at a time when the future is guaranteed to be hard enough as it is.

In portraying realistic futures set during or after times of decline, the stories published in *Into the Ruins* help to counter the first belief of inevitable betterment. But if, in the process, they reinforce the idea that the decline we face will manifest itself in sudden and cataclysmic collapse, then much of the good they might do is mitigated. We need stories that show us both: the hard times ahead and the fact that those hard times will come as they always do, in fits and starts, piecemeal, fractal, chaotic, messy, uneven, and decidedly non-apocalyptic, even if they do feature sudden ends for certain people and places. It's in those sort of messy futures that the actions we can take start to become more clear. It's in those futures that we see our own agency and the ways that, even in troubled times, we can act to better the world.

It also just so happens that the complication, chaos, variability, joy, pain, and myriad human complication found in these kinds of futures makes for, in my opinion, far more interesting stories than those typically found in science fiction these days. Give me not dystopia or apocalypse or space colonization or techno-utopia; give me instead the messiness of humans making their way through a complicated and living world that refuses to conform to their wishes. Those are the stories I want to read and publish.

I imagine that in the future, there will be stories about our time. They will speak of our mistakes and they will probably not speak kindly, especially since they will still be dealing with the fallout from our destructive decisions. They will talk of the decline we went through—the way our civilization came to pieces. Perhaps they will know some of the details and perhaps they won't. I'm not optimistic about the records we'll leave. But I imagine their story, while condensed, will still be long. I do not imagine they'll speak of the day everything fell apart, and if they do, it will be a story of myth, complete with narrative build up, not a literal cataloging of exactly how our world went to pieces.

They will not yearn for the time before our civilization fell, any more than we yearn for the Roman empire. If there are records giving some idea of how we lived, it may interest some, but it will be a curiosity of another time, irrelevant to their lives. We will not be central to future civilizations. If we are known at all, we will be just one more piece of history; one bit of curve on a long arc.

Our civilization's death is certain to be a long one. There's no particular reason to attempt to aggrandize it. It won't be the reference point for all who come after and it won't end the world in a fiery apocalypse. It will simply be one more civilization in a long human history full of them, carrying out its life cycle the way each of billions of humans do, being born, ripening, and eventually dying in the slow, cascading, chaotic way that civilizations die. And then will come another, and another, and another.

The stories to tell are endless: of that death, of all the moments in it, of the civilizations that come afterward, of the complicated path between death and rebirth, of untold humans making their way through fascinating lives on a fascinating planet. Let us tell them. Let us dive into them knowing that now is not the reference point for all, that the future cannot be known in advance, that stories set in decline are as legitimate as stories set in endless progress, that we do not have to hold the reader's hand. Give them reference points, clues, the shadings of a path, detail if it fits the story and vague allusions instead if it doesn't. Let them see the futures we imagine and give them the option to accept those futures or not. But it is in presenting them unapologetically—putting them forth as casually as all those shiny, sterile futures of endless computer technology and easy space travel—that we make them normal. It is in putting them forward over and over and over again—matter of fact, obvious, no labels necessary—that we move from debating if this is the sort of future we can expect, this place of obvious decline when referenced against our now, to debating whether *this* is what the decline might really look like. And it is in placing formed and breathing characters in these worlds, and having them *expect* the world, to know it intimately, to not imagine any other—because why would they? *this is the world*—that we make those futures real, that we change our understanding of what to expect.

And it is *then* that the work begins. Because now we see what to expect, and it's through that knowledge that we begin to understand what we must do.

— Portland, Oregon
March 1, 2018

A Note of Thanks

This issue marks the conclusion of the second year of *Into the Ruins*. It is, so far as I am concerned, quite an achievement. This publication has found a modest but dedicated audience, published forty one pretty damn good stories, paid the authors of those stories, and paid its own bills. It is an effort of love, mind you—my day job remains necessary, no question—but I think that's impressive, especially considering the fact that the theme of *Into the Ruins* is decidedly not mainstream.

There is, of course, only one reason for this success: you readers. Thank you for subscribing, for purchasing issues, for sending in letters to the editor, for voicing your support, for spreading the word.

Over the past two years, I've received a lot of kind words from many of you. More than anything, thank you for that. It means a lot to me, and I hope my responses have made that clear.

Finally, I have a request to make of all of you reading this. Many of you have subscriptions that are ending with this issue. If you haven't renewed yet, please do so now by visiting the web address below. Subscribers are the lifeblood of this publication; if you want us to continue, show your support by reupping your subscription.

And for those of you who aren't subscribers? If you like what you read, consider subscribing. Trust me, it makes a difference. Subscribers keep us going. You can do so at the website below.

Thank you so much for two great years. I'm really looking forward to the third. You all are the best.

— Joel Caris, Editor & Publisher

Subscribe at **intotheruins.com/subscribe**
Renew at **intotheruins.com/renew**

Into the Ruins is published quarterly by Figuration Press. We publish deindustrial science fiction that explores a future defined by natural limits, energy and resource depletion, industrial decline, climate change, and other consequences stemming from the reckless and shortsighted exploitation of our planet, as well as the ways that humans will adapt, survive, live, die, and thrive within this future.

One year, four issue subscriptions to *Into the Ruins* are $39. You can subscribe by visiting intotheruins.com/subscribe or by mailing a check made out to Figuration Press to:

Figuration Press / 3515 SE Clinton Street / Portland, OR 97202

To submit your work for publication, please visit intotheruins.com/submissions or email submissions@intotheruins.com.

All issues of *Into the Ruins* are printed on paper, first and foremost. Electronic versions will be made available as high quality PDF downloads. Please visit our website for more information. The opinions expressed by the authors do not necessarily reflect the opinions of Figuration Press or *Into the Ruins*. Except those expressed by Joel Caris, since this is a sole proprietorship. That said, all opinions are subject to (and commonly do) change, for despite the Editor's occasional actions suggesting the contrary, it turns out he does not know everything and the world often still surprises him.

EDITOR-IN-CHIEF
JOEL CARIS

DESIGNER
JOEL CARIS

WITH THANKS TO
JOHN MICHAEL GREER
SHANE WILSON
CHUCK MASTERSON
OUR SUBSCRIBERS

SPECIAL THANKS TO
KATE O'NEILL

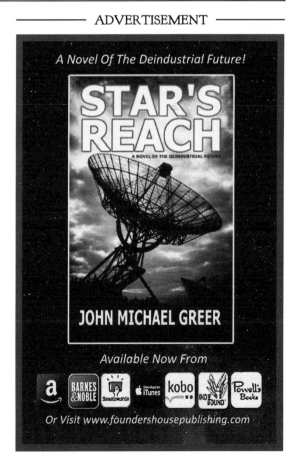

Contributors

JOEL CARIS is a gardener and homesteader, occasional farmer, passionate advocate for local and community food systems, sporadic writer, voracious reader, sometimes prone to distraction and too attendant to detail, a little bit crazy, a cynical optimist, and both deeply empathetic toward and frustrated with humanity. He is your friendly local editor and publisher. As a reader of this journal and perhaps other writings of his, he hopes you don't too easily tire of his voice and perspective. He lives in Oregon with his all-too-amazing wife.

VIOLET BERTELSEN is an herbalist, farmhand and amateur historian currently living in the northeastern United States. While a child, the woods befriended and educated Violet, who proved to be an eager student. She spent her young adulthood in a haze, wandering the vast expanses of North America trying to find the lost fragments of her soul in deserts, hot springs and railyards. Now older and more sedate, she likes to spend her time talking with trees, reading history books, laughing uproariously with fellow farmhands, drinking black birch tea and, on occasion, writing science fiction stories.

ALISTAIR HERBERT writes from a little house on the edge of Todmorden in West Yorkshire, where he lives with his partner and two young children. He studied creative writing at the University of Manchester and now works part time for a local government organisation—an occupation which has largely kept him out of trouble for thirteen years. His work has previously appeared in Comma Press' *Parenthesis* anthology, as well as in *Into the Ruins: Summer 2017* (Issue #6).

CATHERINE MCGUIRE has been writing science fiction since Isaac Asimov gave her encouragement in 1975 in NYC. Her SF publications started with two children's novels for TSR (1984, 1985). Recently her stories have appeared in *Into The Ruins* (Figuration Press) and *MYTHIC* as well as three of the four *After Oil* anthologies (Founders House Publishing). Her deindustrial science fiction novel *Lifeline* is also available from Founders House Publishing. She has four poetry chapbooks and a full-length book of poetry, *Elegy for the 21st Century* (FutureCycle Press). Find her at www.cathymcguire.com.

JUSTIN PATRICK MOORE, KE8COY, is a writer, amateur radio hobbyist and a cataloger at a public library where his curiosity gets him sidetracked into many rabbit holes of reading. His work has been published in *AntenneX*, *Flurb* and *Abraxas: International Journal of Esoteric Studies*. His current writing project explores the historical intersections of electronic music and telecommunications technology. These articles can be found at sothismedias.com. Justin and his wife Audrey make their home in Cincinnati, the Queen of the West.

KL COOKE has been a lifelong reader of fiction, which led him to study literature and creative writing at San Francisco State University. After college, however, he became involved in the electronics industry, working in the Silicon Valley in contracts and project management. After retiring, with a new career taking care of grandchildren, and a growing sense of unease regarding the future, he discovered the "collapsitarian" blogosphere. His earlier interest in writing was renewed, inspired by the works of John Michael Greer and James Howard Kunstler. He is currently working on a novel dealing with life in a post-collapse setting.

W. JACK SAVAGE is a retired broadcaster and educator. He is the author of seven books, including *Imagination: The Art of W. Jack Savage* (wjacksavage.com). To date, more than fifty of Jack's short stories and over seven hundred of his paintings and drawings have been published worldwide. Jack and his wife Kathy live in Monrovia, California. Jack is, as usual, responsible for this issue's cover art.

HOLLY SCHOFIELD travels through time at the rate of one second per second, oscillating between the alternate realities of city and country life. Her short stories have appeared in *Analog*, *Lightspeed*, *Escape Pod*, and many other publications throughout the world. She hopes to save the world through science fiction and homegrown heritage tomatoes. Find her at hollyschofield.wordpress.com.

GRETA HAYER is an MFA student at the University of New Orleans. Her work has appeared in *Pilcrow & Dagger*, *Extract(s)*, and *The Goliard*. Her poem, "Eve," won the Vonna Hicks Adrian prize for poetry in 2016. She received a BA in History from the College of Wooster and currently lives with her cat in New Orleans.

Letters to the Editor

Dear Editor,

It is with sympathy for his family, friends, and the many readers he touched that I write of the passing of Dale Pendell (1947 - January 2018). He was the author of *The Great Bay: Chronicles of the Collapse*, a sweeping future-history of northern California that begins in 2021 and ends ten thousand years later. As you remember, I wrote a review of this book for the first issue of *Into the Ruins*. (Back issues available!) His projections of rising sea levels over geologic time until a great bay has formed over the city of San Francsico were vivid to me, as were the cultures and characters that rose and fell alongside those waters.

I first became aware of Dale's writings through a friend who recommended Dale's *Pharmako* trilogy to me. The three books include *Pharmako/Poeia*, *Pharmako/Dynamis*, and *Pharmako/Gnosis*. In these three books he writes on plants from scientific, poetic, and socio-historical viewpoints, showing how human culture and consciousness have been linked to and shaped by the plants we use and learn from. There is an emphasis on psychoactive plants and herbcraft and what he terms walking the Poison Path. I later read his *The Language of Birds: Some Notes on Chance and Divination.*

Besides his novel of collapse and climate change, another aspect of Dale's work that I became interested in was his concept of Horizon Anarchism. The term came from a 2006 talk he gave at the Palenque Norte theme camp at Burning Man. It delineates a way of building alternative structures now for the creation of a long-term anarchist future that is still on the horizon. It is similar to the counter-cultural notion of "building the new society in the shell of the old." Some of the key ideas of Horizon Anarchism include keeping principles in practice, reforming the existing system, planning for the very long-term, and getting together in an alternative society. A recording of the talk is available online at https://psychedelicsalon.com/podcast-055-horizon-anarchism/

Dale was a prolific author of poetry, founded and edited *Kuksu: Journal of Backcountry Writing*, and wrote a number of other books besides those mentioned above. The spirit of this brave explorer of consciousness will be missed.

Justin Patrick Moore
Cincinnati, Ohio

Dear Editor,

One way that I have tried making the world a better place is in recognizing that each person wakes up to the predicament we are all in at their own pace, and people who are asleep in the dream of perpetual techno-nirvana don't want to have their dreaming interrupted by nagging ideologues. When people complain about the current state of politics, I tell them "Don't fight against it, just disregard it all." Instead, replace that energy you would use in resistance with a positive vision of yourself creating some worthy goal, whatever your talents and inclination would support, and then work towards that vision. Pull yourself into your vision of the future through your own effort.

In my own case, being trained in ecology and the building trades, I decided to build tiny homes as a way to create habitable shelters that used minimal resources, and work in greater harmony with natural energy flows. During the design phase, I am mindful of ways in which the dwelling could be adapted currently, or in the future, to utilize an even lower level of technology. A few examples are: replacing a propane hot air heater with a rocket mass stove, or replacing an instant hot water heater with a breadbox solar hot water heater, or replacing PV and inverter-powered AC lighting with DC lighting.

A simpler future is within reach of each individual, if they choose.

Stephen Treimel
Carrboro, North Carolina

Dear Editor,

Thank you for *Into the Ruins No. 7*. I appreciate the help it gives me as I try to imagine what is coming.

Several authors imagine life in newly-warmed areas of the far north or south. Will anyone dare to imagine what survival might look like in the tropics after another century of climate change?

Your points about self-driving cars are right on target. I suppose another justification of them is that they'll alleviate the tedium of commuting and allow us to be "productive" as we travel. Of course, that productivity will probably consist in wasting time online—and as we stop driving, we will lose our connections to the landscape and our bodily understanding of automotive technology.

A rival for most absurd technological idea is the "smart speaker," which has actually gotten much farther. Millions now own devices that place their homes under constant surveillance by would-be-monopolistic corporations, and chat with algorithms as if they really understood human words. You won't catch me doing it.

Carry on and best wishes,

Richard Polt
Cincinnati, Ohio
sent from his 1942 Woodstock 5N
typewriterrevolution.com

Dear Editor,

I am much obliged to your recent correspondent, one C. Masterson: first for supplying me with fresh ammunition, and second for his tendering what was, doubtless, well-meant advice. I was surprised to find so learned a scholar recommending unconditional surrender to vulgar usage; however, tastes differ. Mine, sir, is to stand fast in the face of common folly. Let it be so that one supports a Lost Cause; is that any reason to give up the good fight? No, I say. Hang on to your Roman numerals, boys—the Ablative shall rise again!

Can Bachelor Masterson be unaware of the Doctrine of Dominoes? If we, the noble Few, succumb to the nescient rabble on the sacred grounds of proper pluralization, other parts of speech will be swept beneath an evil tide. Already the ignorant mob lays siege to the rightful rulership of possessive its; substituting their ill-considered contraction for the phrase 'it is'; it's, indeed! Like a king deposed by a crownéd donkey, is our its.

Think, sir! Shall we stand meekly aside as this rampant plague of apostrophes infests our limited supply of possessive pronouns? Shall I live to see his become hi's, hers become her's and ours become (shudder) ours's?

Never! Never, say I! Not while life and breath and typography endure!

If The Many (some certainly unwashed; though I must say I have met quite a number of Dirty Birds among The Few, especially those who forswear the splendid oratory of Seneca and Cicero to wallow in the bawdy muck and low amusements proffered by Catuluus and Martial—but, I digress) are allowed to corrode plurals with their salt sea of lowering ignorance, how, sir, shall the shining swords of conceptual discrimination endure? Bright metal must be polished, sharp edges must be continually renewed.

The creeping corruption of base wit and murky mental mush are no fit exchange for the brilliant ring of civil converse, nor the diamond of discerning thought. No, sir: I do not stand down. I am but one soldier in a great war. I cannot defend every arena now threatened by the rising powers of the Vulgate; but, as a data steward, it is my duty to maintain the purity of my plurals, written or spoken, subjectively, subjunctively, objectively, datively, and indubitably. Sauce from the improper geese is souse for the propaganda.

Sincerely,

G.Kay Bishop
Durham, North Carolina

Dear Readers,

In my Editor's Introduction, I wrote about how change often unfolds over time. I spoke of some of my own personal changes, but not in great detail. However, it is here in the letters pages where I most hope to see the hashing out of new ways to live, of my readers debating strategies, changes, habits, attitudes, and experiments that may serve to guide us through the troubled times of today and the future. Therefore, I want to write a moment about some of the changes of habit and experimentation taking place in my own household over the past year, in the hopes of both encouraging new practices among those reading this and encouraging the submission of letters in which readers talk of their own lives and the efforts they're making.

Some of my new and burgeoning habits are small. I am taking navy showers in the new year, for instance: turning the water off to soap up so as to save water and the electricity that heats it.

Others are a learning process. I purchased a Tayama fireless cooker last year and recently pulled it out from the basement to finally begin experimenting with it, along with my wife. For those who are unfamiliar, a fireless cooker is a simple, highly-insulated chamber with a pot and lid that fit inside it. You use it by bringing something you want to cook to a boil in the provided pot for a few minutes and then transferring the pot from the stove top to the insulated chamber.

The heat is retained with very minimal heat loss in the insulated chamber, which continues the cooking process without the need for additional energy. Our experimentation with the device has yielded mixed results: using it to make stock has been a definite success while our attempts to cook rice in it and a soup with wheat berries were less than satisfactory. I am curious to try other soups and perhaps even a pot roast, and I imagine greater experimentation would lead to greater success. In the meantime, I've found a way to make stock while using far less energy, as well as to do it in the summer with less inadvertent heating of our small apartment. That feels like a win, even if small.

Other changes are ones we have built to over time. Hang drying our laundry is one of those. When we moved into our apartment together, I would hang dry most of our laundry during the summer. During last winter, however, we mostly transitioned to using the dryer, though I would watch the weather and hang dry as possible. This winter has been a different story. With the help of a used wooden drying rack we purchased off the sidewalk for five dollars and the discovery that button down shirts placed on hangers can be hung off our 1920s-era picture railing, we have transitioned to drying the majority of our laundry indoors during the winter, without use of the electric dryer. Hung in front of and near our natural gas wall heater, our laundry typically dries in a day or so, making the task feasible with some basic planning. Towels and sheets still sometimes end up in the dryer, but a little experimentation with hangers and monitoring of the weather has allowed me to hang dry those multiple times, as well. All told, I suspect we've cut a good ninety percent of our dryer usage.

Meanwhile, we continue to work to reduce our driving time. Upon moving in together, my wife and I eliminated one of our cars, going down to a shared one. That not only served to place additional limits on our driving, but it saved us money, too. Since then, my wife has increased the frequency of her walks and bus rides to work, to the point that she now rarely commutes by car. I still have to commute from Portland to the coast occasionally for my job, but otherwise I almost never use the car during the week; multiple grocery stores, a hardware store, the post office, the library, and plenty more (not to mention bars, restaurants, a couple movie theaters, and a variety of specialty shops) are all within a very reasonable (about two miles or less) walking distance, and so I walk my errands, as well as a good amount of my entertainment.

I could go on (there are other changes, and I haven't even talked about my favorite one: food!) but I imagine you all get the point. There are many ways to live a simpler life and help create a better future for ourselves and others, as Stephen Treimel notes in his letter. All it takes is a choice, a willingness, and some basic knowledge or creativity. Hearing what others are doing often helps, as well, and I hope *Into the Ruins* readers will consider sending in letters about the changes and experimentation in their own lives. There are rich conversations to be had here, and an endless number of more satisfying ways to live. Let's do our small part to foster them.

Joel Caris, Editor
Portland, Oregon

Into the Ruins welcomes letters to the editor from our readers. We encourage thoughtful commentary on the contents of this issue, the themes of the magazine, and humanity's collective future. Readers may email their letters to editor@intotheruins.com or mail them to:

Figuration Press
3515 SE Clinton Street
Portland, OR 97202

Please include your full name, city and state, and an email or phone number. Only your name and location will be printed with any accepted letter.

STORIES

PROPHECY

BY GRETA HAYER

AFTER FIVE NIGHTS OF TRAVEL ON THE ROAD OF THE OLD GODS, the fortress known as the Nest could be seen poking up from the horizon like some kind of animal trap. The roads leading to it, including the one we were on, crisscrossed and wove as though they were threads tied in a great knot—not concrete, massive structures, yellowed by time. The Nest rose out of the dry fields, towers poking through the tangle of roads. The palace at the heart of the structure was unseeable, but I peered at the fortress through the dim light, hoping my new home would be as beautiful as I had heard.

I noticed Blair, his head pointed toward the Nest but his eyes on my lap, counting my fingers for what had to be the thousandth time. It wasn't his fault he was so obvious about it. He was a warrior, as evidenced by the missing finger on his left hand. He had never been taught things like numbers, no more than was necessary. So when he looked at my hands and moved his lips wordlessly, feeling the shape of each number if not the sound, I could tell he was counting.

When he looked up, my eyes were on him, narrowed in a way that I hoped seemed cool and disconcerting. I had long ago learned to wield the power of my gaze, of my mismatched eyes. One green, one brown. Seer's eyes. They weren't the kind of eyes you wanted on you for very long. I saw Blair fidget, his broad, slow face pinching with anxiety. He looked away. Eventually, I did too, letting him go. If he was afraid of me, he wouldn't hurt me.

The oxen plodded us closer to the Nest. It was slow going, and, this time of year, we could only travel at night. Even night this far south was hot, but at least there was no pounding sun in our faces. Neither of us was tanned enough to handle the sun anyway. Blair was from farther north than me, and his skin was red with blisters from just the few hours he spent in the evening light.

I couldn't tell if Blair was suspicious or just superstitious, but his finger counting settled uneasy in my mind. Certainly, he was afraid of me, and I was mildly proud of that, and it was difficult to consider that a man who could barely count to ten could have seen something in me that King Kross himself couldn't. My old king was sharp, but he was more like a ball passed between his advisors, his opinions and favors slipping away to yield to whichever advisor held him the tightest. He barely had time to think for himself, let alone think about me. I tried to summon up the visage of my old king, but even after such a short time, his face shifted in my memory. I couldn't remember what he looked like, only the masks that he wore. Angry, selfish, compassionate, remorseful. How many kings had I dealt with, all with the same name? He had given me fine clothes and a chamber with lace curtains, but when I had begged for his protection, he reminded me that a seer was still a slave. Even the memory of that conversation made shame and anger twist my belly. I took a deep breath. I had escaped, hadn't I? And this new place, the Nest. It had to be better, right? At least the bad man couldn't follow me here.

We approached the Nest, the hot wind in our faces, arriving sweaty and sticky just before dawn. I could see why they called it the Nest. The structure was surrounded by layers, the outermost being the roads themselves, looking like clovers, cutting over and under. They made me think of ribbons—huge, concrete ribbons. They were so big that they made the hollow of my stomach echo like a cavern.

After the roads of the old gods were the gateways. Before each one, piles of timber and poles of iron criss-crossed the roads so that any traveler was slowed if not stopped. The Nest was a fortress, first and foremost, and as we picked our way through the mostly impassible landscape, Blair jumping off the cart frequently to move a pole or shove a boulder out of the way, I watched the gateways themselves, tall and imposing. They reminded me of a man's fingers as he tries to claw his way out of the dirt. The doors were small, and I wondered if we would have to walk the rest of the way, but our cart fit through the tiny arch. No one manned the gateway we passed through. No one needed to.

Behind the gates was the bramble, and it reminded me of war. Steel spikes, concrete barricades, and filth. Trash, plastic, everything old and dirty. There were hundreds of white boxes, the big kind that the old ones had used to store food. I used to know the old word for them, but I couldn't think of it now. King Kross had repurposed them as coffins, and I wondered if this king had as well. All through the bramble and possible graveyard, rusting staircases made of slender strips of metal zigzagged in contorted positions, like the bones of an animal who had died in pain. They had rusted red and brown. It would be easy for someone to get caught here, pinned somehow on the thorny debris and trapped.

The bright dawn burst through the bramble, spearing through the darkness. The sunrise might have been beautiful once, but it was white hot and dangerous now. Coming from behind the Nest, the light seemed to splinter like a million piercing weapons, merciless, brutal, and beautiful. In the great war that killed the old gods, there were lights so bright that they had toppled buildings, or at least that was what the eleven-fingered scholars told us. White heat that left charred shadows on walls, hotter than flame or noontime sun or anything we children of gods could imagine.

A shiver ran up my spine, the feverish shiver of fear. A kind of self-loathing spread from it, a reddening shame. I had done this to myself. Foolishly, I had left King Kross for this place of filth and fear. I had chosen to leave my pretty chambers with their curtains and marble. I had become afraid of them. I wanted to laugh at myself in the kind of mirthless way someone does when they should be dead or wanted to be. In my memory, I saw a gloved hand behind those floating curtains, then the delicate, songlike sound of the filigree tearing into a long, ugly gash.

I stopped the memory, my sweat like ice on my skin. I was not foolish to have come here. I had to leave, and here was the place I had maneuvered and manipulated myself to get to. This journey was a testament to my abilities as a seer and as an advisor. I should have been proud of myself, not haunted with fear. No other woman would have been able to escape like me. And escape I did. Five nights of distance was enough that no man would chase me. And I had the king's blessing and his guard at my side. I was a slave in name alone, for no slave had dreamed of the power I had taken for myself.

Blair and I stopped at a second set of gates, and three guards emerged from hidden crannies, their left hands open and ungloved. Twenty seven fingers between them. "Who are you?" one asked. He wore tough, lightweight armor over his chest, but kept his tan arms free. His face was all but covered with a thin linen cloth, much like my own veil.

"Siggy, Seer of King Kross of the Midland Wastes, and my guard, Blair Ninefingers." My voice rang out clearly and confidently. I had always been good at acting.

The guards gathered together, and I saw that all three had guns. This king must have been a wealthy man indeed, though the skeptical part of me wondered if the guards had a single bullet between them. Ammo, rarer every year, was perhaps the dearest thing that money could buy. A single round might have paid for my chains and servitude, perhaps Blair's as well. I doubted that the morning patrol had such luxuries. Regardless, I moved slowly and languorously. It was no good dying for stupidity.

"Welcome to the Southern Flats, Siggy Seer," a guard said, meeting my gaze for just long enough to authenticate my identity. Only seers had eyes like mine. He waved us past, and when we emerged from the gate, I saw the palace of the southern king, glittering mirror-like. A thousand facets reflected a thousand colors of dawn, colors I hadn't considered to belong to the sky or the earth. Colors beyond pink and red and yellow. I conjured up long-lost words, the kind of words that nobody but the scribes used anymore: rose, salmon, scarlet, blush, peach, magenta, champagne . . . It was beautiful, its glistening towers, its arches and peaks, every surface covered with the thin, hard Apples of the old ones.

It was at this sight when I learned how very rich the southern king had to be. To have covered his palace in gold would have been easier. Apples were rarer, a sign of status despite their uselessness. No one really knew what the Apples had been used for, back when the gods walked in the place of men. Even my teacher, her old, mismatched eyes lighting up, had spoken of the worlds behind the glass, places in this world but also others. With the Apples, the touch of a button could summon the voices of gods. But, other times, my teacher told me of endless information, stories from all over the world, reported to the Apples as soon as it had happened. I had trouble believing all this to be true. My teacher hadn't been in full control of her mind at the end. Her prophecies and her histories had blended in a way that made them impossible to distinguish, like fate woven in endless circles. She had predicted that one day, all us children of the gods would speak into the rectangular faces of the Apples and hear voices from across the boiling sea.

My mouth hung open and my eyes lifted wide. I blinked, but that briefest moment when my lids covered my vision made me doubt the wealth and beauty from the moment before. When I opened my eyes, I was once again shocked and delighted. I had never imagined that such a structure could have been created by the children of the gods and not the old gods themselves.

Blair snorted. "Surely you foresaw all this?"

I closed my mouth and tried to sound stately and mystic. "There are some visions that cannot be truly seen in clear water."

Blair nodded, pretending to understand, and I considered this punishment enough for doubting me.

We were taken into the palace of old Apples, four guards on either side. I tried to get a glimpse of the Apples closer up, but their flat faces revealed no secrets of inner worlds. The inside of the palace was cool, despite the growing day, and there were servants in every corner, waving the air through the hallways with huge, woven fans. We came to a room with a mosaic door with the image of one of the great mushroom clouds, and inside that door was the king.

He wasn't a tall man, but his presence in the room was so grand, I knew him to be King Marro at once. He wore layers of cloth so light that it seemed to be crafted from air. He had gold around his temples and neck and in his ears; otherwise, he was an image in pure, unbroken white. Even his skin was pale as ivory, without so much as a freckle to show unwanted sun exposure. When I entered the room, his brown eyes narrowed, appraising me for a short yet significant moment. Then his face brightened, and he clapped his hands together. To the nobles and advisors in the room, he said, "The seer has arrived," and to me, "We have been waiting for you."

I bowed, trying to seem sagelike, but the exhaustion of travel was settling on my bones. I was dirty and sweaty and hot, and my linen shift was wrinkled and covered with stains and streaks of grime. I was not fit to be seen or smelled by anyone. I quickly scanned the room. Twelve men, all free from deformity, except the scribe, but that was to be expected. Who was dangerous? I picked out a tall man with a goatee and a wide one with arms thick as some people's legs. But neither one leered at me with sticky eyes. Perhaps the situation would change once I cleaned up, but for now, I was safe. A giddy smile tugged at my mouth, but I pressed my lips together. If they were scared of me, they wouldn't touch me, and no one would be scared of a girl who laughed with a kind of drunken disbelief before the king.

"Thank you, my king," I said. "I am happy to find the Nest as beautiful and formidable as I have heard." I had been hoping to say something about generosity or kindness for the sake of flattery and suggestion, but my teacher's last command guided my words. In my memory, her gnarled whisper was as clear as it had been when she spoke upon her death bed. *Don't lie.* There was nothing kind or generous about my journey here. Just hot, flat plains with barely a copse for shade. Even the land had been stingy.

The king hardly seemed to notice my words. Instead, he waved forward a serving girl with a large, shallow bowl of carved stone. Dread filled my belly as the king spoke. "A reading of the waters, my seer, to welcome you to my lands."

Don't ever read for a person before you know them, my teacher's voice filled my head again. *Learn who they are first: more than a few foolish seers were put to death on the spot because they made themselves the bearers of bad news to kings who couldn't hear it.*

I ran through a dozen excuses in my mind, but the simplest won out. *Don't lie.* "My king, I will be happy to read for you tonight. However, traveling so far has left me drained. I fear I would be blind to anything in the waters but a warm bath and a soft bed."

The king nodded, but his face screwed into a frustrated frown. "Very well, then. Tonight."

I was dismissed, and chatter like nervous birds arose from the courtiers. I wondered if the king would send me back North with Blair if he didn't like what I had to say. Likely, he would simply kill me. I might have been more valuable than other servants, but I was his to do with as he pleased, bought and traded for. Three carts of oranges each month of the harvest for the span of five years. Few people ever learned of their worth as plainly as I had.

The serving girl set down the heavy bowl with a slight sigh of relief. At least I had pleased one person.

I was given rooms on the southern side of the palace. The brightest side, but everything was so magnificent that I wasn't bothered to complain about the light, even to myself. Granite floors cool to the touch, curtains that blocked the light, even a servant who moved the petals of a large fan with a bicycle-like contraption. I dismissed her after my bath, and she drained the grey water from the tub and left me alone. Wrapped in a silk robe, I stood by the windows for a time, one long beam of daylight slipping from between the curtains. *I can be happy here*, I told myself. *Can't I?* King Marro seemed to treat me like a dignitary more than a slave, and none of the advisors in the court looked at me like I was prey. I had done the right thing, hadn't I? If that was true, why did I still feel trapped?

What would my teacher have said to me now? Would she be disappointed that I had abandoned our king? She had been like a grandmother to Kross, and everyone in his castle had treated her with such respect. How could she have anticipated that everything would change after her death? I wondered if she was a very good seer at all. Wouldn't she have tried to protect me? Would she have been able to? I sighed. No, the only safety for a woman was to be valuable to a man. To be pregnant, to be rich, or to be magic. When my teacher died, I wondered what would happen if I carved out my green eye and took up another life, but then I watched an ewerer in Kross's palace get an infection in his eye. They sent him to the pigsties. One eyed folk were to be swineherds, no matter who they were before.

I tried to sleep in the tall bed, but it was so much softer than the floor of the cart had been during the journey that I felt suffocated by it rather than comforted. Flighty, anxious dreams chased me like shadows. The Nest and its spiky layers, a dawn as red as a pumping heart, and, in the distance, a great mushroom cloud and an endless, unforgiving summer.

I must have eventually slept, for, when I woke at last, shivering and sticky all over again, there was a plate of fruit lit by several long candles. It was well past dusk, and time for me to be concocting a vision of the future for my new king, a task made even more difficult by the visions of the past ensnared by my subconscious. I crawled out of bed, my body stiff in the way that comes from sleeping too long, and I tiptoed to the food. Oranges, yes, I knew those, though less than my tongue would have liked. But besides oranges, half a dozen other fruits (if they were fruits at all) lay arranged in concentric circles on a large glass plate. I wondered at their names. There was a fruit with flesh so yellow that I wondered if it could be poisonous. Another was like a sickle moon in both shape and color but tasted nothing like I would expect from the night sky. One tan oval led to my discovery of a new nut. Peanut? I had heard stories of them, always children's food, but it tasted adult enough to me. I was very full and feeling like an accomplished detective when I leaned back in the armed chair and gazed out of the windows. The lower levels of the Nest twinkled, candles making the sprawling flatlands mimic the spangled sky above. I couldn't see the fearsome layers, painted in the colors of dawn. There were figures moving in the distance, but they were too far away to read any malice. Guards, travelers, merchants, or perhaps simply lightning bugs.

I let out a breath, and it seemed to have contained the stress of weeks. I was safe here, I told myself, despite the dreams and despite my pending vision for the king. There were no more sneaking predators. No one was going to hurt me here. No one was going to hurt me again.

I jumped at a sound, but it was only the door opening. A servant? No, I decided immediately. The woman who walked into my chamber was nothing like a servant. Tall, with hair that curled like a cascading waterfall, she moved into my room like it belonged to her. She held her dainty chin up, her black eyes finding me with calm authority. She was the most beautiful woman I had ever seen. Something seized my stomach, an emotion that could have been jealousy, anger, or even lust, while, at the same time, I felt the urge to withdraw, to hide. I was small and ugly and awkward. I was nothing compared to her, and we were close enough in age that it was impossible to resist comparison.

She smiled. "I hope I did not disturb you, Seer Siggy," she said in a voice like cool water. "I only heard that you were awake, and I wanted to speak with you."

She wanted me to tell her her future, that's what she would have said, but I'd be a worthless seer if I needed her to ask aloud. I smiled a bit. I could do this. She had already told me everything I needed to know. Her painted nails, red as a cherry, her perfect hair, her long orange dress, smooth and fitted to her elegant height.

"You are the Princess Dido, daughter of King Philip, brought here to be wed to King Marro." Even in King Kross's land we had heard tales of her beauty, and the betrothal had scared my king—an alliance so strong and not so very far away. It had made it easier to arrange my escape to this place. I could keep both a mundane and a witch eye on things.

Dido was smiling at me, a small one, but a dimple appeared on one cheek. Adorable. "Indeed I am," she said, and I felt a familiar surge of pride in myself. I was a seer, regardless of any gift or lack thereof.

I made the other observations necessary. The lack of the wedding band on her finger told me that the ceremony hadn't gone through yet. The stiffness in her jaw that told me she was uncomfortable, possibly scared. But the darting of those black, black eyes and the way her throat quivered in the candle light showed me the same emotion that I covered up with bravado every night: the look of someone long hunted, stressed to the point of breaking but unable to break. My feelings of envy over her beauty began to ebb. We were the same, the princess and I. We both were slaves to kings in our own ways, both *merely* women, with so little agency over our own lives. I nearly felt pity for her. For all her beauty and fame, she had less power over her life than I had. At least I had chosen to come here. She had been sold just as easily, but without the carefully planned and terribly influential visions I had used to guide my old master's hand. I felt much less small.

"You will lead a hard life," I said. *Don't lie.*

"I know that," Dido snapped, and my confidence shattered. "None of that bullshit. Tell me what will happen if I carry through with my plan."

What plan? I was immediately suspicious. What kinds of plans did beautiful princesses concoct? To kill the king on their wedding night? It was so very classic and so very stupid that for a moment I lost my admiration for her. But as I opened my mouth to allude to a knife in a bedroom, I stopped. She wasn't a killer, not with a knife at the very least. She was sly like a cat, letting you pet her only to find her teeth sunk into your hand. She was a poisoner, a quiet assassin. I shivered, then berated myself. She had probably never killed anyone and had no plans to, I told myself. I was just being paranoid.

"You haven't seen anything, have you?" Dido said with disappointment in her voice.

"I have not yet done a reading in the Southern Flats."

One of her eyebrows twitched.

I felt small and ugly again. "I will consider your question when I consult the waters for the king," I said.

Another twitch, but this time it was her lips. "Very well, then." She played with a small red bead of fruit left on my breakfast tray. I hadn't tasted it. I wasn't even sure I could call it a fruit. She plucked one from the mound and placed it delicately on her tongue. It made a popping sound in her mouth. A droplet of red juice escaped to settle on her lower lip.

She glanced at the half-eaten fruit tray, as if answering a question I hadn't asked. "Pomegranate," she said. "You should try it. It's good." But her tone made it sound as though it tasted like acid.

She began to leave but paused, her back to me, in the doorway. One of her long -fingered hands clutched the door frame, and her orange dress spilled onto the floor like a sunset. Was she aware of how beautiful she was in that moment, her head half turned, her eyes sharp?

"The king is mad," she said. "Be careful."

For my Seeing for the king, the room was arranged with so many candles it looked and felt as though I had stepped out at high noon. I immediately regretted the robe I had chosen, thick and regal but too warm for proximity to such fire.

The king wore white again, and he seemed to gleam, so clean were his garments. His guards stood ready at the edge of the room, matched in orange. A row of nobles or advisers stood opposite the guards. Dido stood among them, though she had changed out of her sunset-colored gown for a simpler green. Blair, too, stood between Marro's guards and the onlookers, which surprised me. I had forgotten about him. When would he be sent back to King Kross? An eleven-fingered scribe stood nearby, ready to record the occasion.

Everyone was looking at me.

My belly flipped, but I kept a calm expression on my face. With as much stately sagacity as I could muster, I walked to the center of the room and bowed low to the king. "If it pleases you, my king, I shall attempt to peer into the future for you."

"It would please me very much." He had a voice that seemed too high to belong to a man, more like a boy. He seemed . . . soft. Not mad, but not like the savage merchant king rumor suggested. I tried to look at him, but his robes seemed so blindingly white that I had to turn away.

I took two steps toward the thing that I had been avoiding looking at. A pedestal, a thin tall table, and the shallow basin of water that weighed heavily upon it. I felt like I carried that basin in my arms as I approached, my steps leaden and loud, though I only wore thin sandals. And then I arrived at the platform. One step up. One step, but it seemed like I moved the whole sky with me. I brought the other foot up, and the silence of the room began to press on me so I felt as though I was being crushed from all angles by men with guns and advisors with frowns, and by the weight of the world itself. The king, in the corner of my eye, looked like a pillar of flame, the whitest, hottest part of a fire. I swallowed, and the pressure of the world forced my head down, so that there was nothing I could do but stare into the smooth water.

And, of course, there was nothing to see there.

Maybe the old ones had had gifts for future telling. Stories said that they could read when storms would come or if actions would bear consequences. Maybe, even, the old ones with different colored eyes could see things in still water. But if it were true, the technology or knowledge had been lost. I didn't have any magical ability, just a lucky malformation of my irises. And so, like a man without a finger becomes a warrior or a woman with webbed toes is taught to fish, I had been brought to King Kross's old seer to be trained in the sight. Charlatan, imposter, fraud: my teacher never needed to say those words aloud for me to realize there was no sense to the castes, just chance. A skinny, flimsy child born with nine fingers still had a role to play, whether he was a good warrior or not.

"What do you see?" the king prompted, eagar and impatient. Something about such childishness in a full grown man unnerved me. I couldn't read him at all. Was this a game to him, or did my life hang in the balance?

Don't lie, I reminded myself. "I see a nest in a great fruit tree. Women emerge from the fruits but do not go back in. I see a king, burning like the hottest part of a flame, a fire that is him, though it may also consume him, if he is not careful. I see a sunrise red as blood and as beautiful as they were in the times of the old gods."

I looked up, suddenly exhausted. Was that enough? It was dramatic, and what was a seer if not some kind of entertainment? A boring seer is worse than a bad one, my teacher used to say. My vision had warning and truth, both compelling. It had darkness and light, which made it hard to prove wrong. I didn't know exactly what I'd meant by it all, but meaning could be found underneath the symbolism. I looked toward the king.

True fear, not the nervousness or anxiety I'd felt earlier, washed through me. He was smiling, not the smile of mirth or joy but a cruel, wolf-grin of a smile, like he was about to eat me whole. Behind him, Dido had a hand on her chest, as if trying to hold onto her heart.

The king began to laugh, and I took a step backwards, forgetting I was on the raised pedestal. I teetered, and then, for a moment, I was falling through nothingness. I hit the hard ground on my tailbone, and the pain shot up my back.

The king claimed my empty space on the pedestal, not even seeming to notice my fall. With both hands, he pushed the basin, overturning it onto the floor. The water swelled out, dampening me as I sat, stunned, too scared to move. The basin clattered on the floor and split cleanly into two pieces. The water was cold, and it reflected the candles in the room and contorted the faces of the witnesses until they looked stretched and deformed as hot wax.

I didn't know how long I lay there, soaking slowly to the bone. People flowed out of the room around me like I was a rock in a river. I wanted to be sick. I had shown myself as weak, as frightened. Now everyone here would see me as the seer fallen in the puddle, not a powerful woman capable of changing lives with her visions. I had just gotten here, and I was ruined already.

After some time, all was quiet but the whispers of the candles and the patter of the dripping water. Then Dido was beside me, helping me to stand. Her face was like the moon on a cloudless night. I gasped at the sheer, simple beauty of her, as natural and unstoppable as mountains reaching toward the sky.

"You fool," she whispered. "Did you not know of the last prophecy?"

I shook my head.

"He said the king would drop a candle and burn himself alive."

I swallowed. "What happened to the seer?"

She shook her head.

I felt sick. I leaned against the wall, suddenly weak again.

"Siggy?"

In a voice barely louder than a breath, I said a private prophecy to her. "Your plan. It will only succeed if you take me with you."

‡‡

"We should take your guard with us," Dido said. We were in her chambers, rooms of such elegance that they could only be for her. From the candelabras to the paintings, the rooms were filled with things from the old gods. She had books, though only scribes were taught to read, and a mirror in a golden frame. I hadn't seen a mirror so large and untarnished. I had never seen myself so clearly in my life. The mirror reflected the room and the two of us, sitting cross legged on her bed. In the reflection, the dark haired woman seemed relaxed, effortless, and stunning. The woman with the hair like sand looked tired, gawky, and plain. I turned away from the mirror, focusing on the princess.

"Blair? He would not betray his king."

"Which king?"

"Kross."

"You don't think we'd be safer with a man?" Dido leaned forward, placing her chin in her hand. Her littlest finger brushed against the corner of her lips absently.

"No." We didn't need a man to escape. We could do this just the two of us. Besides, what if Blair went to Marro with our plans? What would the mad king do to us? I thought of the white boxes nestled in the bramble outside. Did Marro use them as coffins as well? And what would he do to us before he killed us? That was the more frightening part. Would we be tortured? Given to his guards? Would Dido still be dragged to his bed, wedding or not? I thought of her soft ivory flesh and how easily it would bruise. I couldn't let that happen to her.

"No men," I said.

"Do you say that as a seer?" Her eyebrow raised. Did she know I was a fraud?

"I say it as someone who has escaped a court before. We don't need him." I didn't want to have to tell her my story, but I would if it would convince her. I didn't want to tell her the things that men were capable of.

I changed the subject. "What will you do when we get out?" As far as I could tell, she was perfect, not a single deformity. If she had been born in a city and not as a king's daughter, she could have done whatever she wanted with her life.

"I think I'd like to be a candlemaker." She smiled at the thought. "I like bees."

I almost laughed at the image of the princess tending to a sticky hive in one of her expensive silk dresses, but, in some ways, the profession suited her. I could imagine her creating scents and colors for the candles, plying the warm wax with her hands.

"And I could still eat honey," she said, excited. "It will be hard to give up all these comforts, but as long as I can still have honey . . ."

I smiled. Sweetness welled in my mouth at the thought. Dido eating honey. Dido licking it off her fingers. I felt a trickle of sweat run down my spine.

I reached for a fan and waved it at my face. The moving air seemed to help, but I still felt flushed.

"What will you do?" she asked.

I swallowed, collecting myself. "I don't know." Swineherd or seer? Or was there a king I could serve who would trust and protect me? "I will walk for a while. West, I think. I want to see what lies beyond the southern flats."

Dido nodded. "West is a fine way to go. North and west is my father's land." She tugged at a silver ring on her hand. "If you go his way, give him this, and tell him how you helped me."

I took the ring, and it was warm to the touch. "Thank you."

She smiled but said nothing for a long time. I sat there too, wordlessly fanning myself. I needed to leave, to go back to my room. I needed to prepare for the trip, to sleep well, to eat a big meal, but I didn't want to leave. Then I caught a glimpse of our reflection in Dido's mirror.

"Good day," I said, slipping off the bed. "I'll see you at sunset."

We picked through the brambles of the Nest toward the city behind it, and my bag snagged on a rusty spoke. I made a little sound, freeing it, but stumbled loudly into a metal staircase.

"Shhh," Dido said, two steps behind me. "If they catch us, we're as good as dead."

I knew that. Of course I knew that. I looked back at the palace, glittering in the moonlight with its many Apples. Dido was pale, her red lips pressed into a thin line. It would be dawn soon, and our escape would be much harder in the heat of the day. She was lucky to have me with her. I blazed the trail through the rubble, and I had packed our two bags. Hers held food and water. Mine held tools, a tent, and the things we would need to set up our new lives. I let her take the lighter one. She was a princess after all, or candlemaker, I supposed. Candlemaker, and not the bride of the mad king. I felt a swell of pride. I had saved her. I reminded myself of my observation when she had first come to my room. Yes, she was a princess and rich and beautiful, but I had so much more power to influence my life. I had escaped the bad man in King Kross's court, hadn't I? Now I was helping her escape a similar evil. She needed me.

And me? Something in my belly buzzed like Dido's bees. It took me a long time to recognize that that feeling was hope. I was scared, but the quivering in my gut tasted like honey, not fear.

There was a crunch behind us, the sound of a boot sinking through metal and mud. I turned. A shadowy figure obscured the lights from the palace. Broad shouldered, tall. A scream bubbled in my throat, but I held it back.

"Dido?" The voice was deep and familiar.

"Blair, I'm glad you could find us."

Something cold seemed to wind its way around my belly. "I thought we agreed no men," I hissed.

Dido looked back at me, her eyes the same color as the night. I thought she would say something, but she just stood there, a shadow blending into the darkness. Blair came closer, each step slow and heavy, until he stood just behind Dido.

"How do you think we got out of the palace so easily? Blair set a distraction." She shrugged off her bag and handed it to him. His eyes followed her movement like a dumb puppy. Poor Blair. He was in love with her. When had she seduced him? Had she left her chambers yesterday after we finished plotting and gone to him? What had she promised him?

Behind them, dawn's first fingers touched the surface of the palace, refracting into the sky. It shone as yellow as the eye of a flame. I squinted. No, it wasn't yellow as a flame. It *was* a flame. The palace was on fire.

"We must hurry," Dido said, glancing at the palace as well. I watched her throat vibrate as she swallowed. She took a step past me. "I'm sorry."

Blair seized me from behind, his arms as hard as steel. Something inside of me shattered. I thought I would scream and claw at him. I thought I would rake my fingernails across his eyes. I wanted to fight, to kill if need be, but my body had gone limp. It was as though my mind and body had been disconnected, that the rag doll in Blair's grip wasn't me. It couldn't have been me.

"What should we do with her?" Blair asked.

Dido didn't look at us, but turned away from the Nest.

"You're not a very good seer, are you, Siggy?" Dido said. How long had she suspected I was a fraud? Since our first meeting? Since the vision for the king? "You were right about one thing, though. I couldn't have done it without you."

I screamed, but Blair's hand muffled it. He shifted, pulling me off my feet, moving me through the sludge. Why couldn't I move?

"Put her here," Dido said, and opened the lid of one of the white boxes. A reek, ungodly and putrid, wafted out. No, not there. The old ones had called them fridges, I remembered, though the name for such a thing seemed useless now. I didn't want my mind coming up with forgotten vocabulary, but it didn't seem to matter what I wanted. *Fridge*, my mind thought of its own accord. *What a cold word.*

Blair began to lower me into the box, and I bit down hard on his hand. At the very least, he would be Blair Eightfingers when I was done with him. His blood tasted like salt and dirt. It tasted a lot like my own blood. I gagged.

I was shoved down, and the lid closed. I heard something heavy placed on top of it, so heavy I was afraid it would break though the box and kill me. A stupid thing to be afraid of, I realized. I was going to die here. Maybe it would have been better if it was quick.

In the total darkness and near complete silence, I spat Blair's finger out of my mouth.

I thought of my last prophecy. A nest and a red sun. Women emerging from sticky-sweet cages. And a king burning.

I hadn't been so wrong after all.

THE CHANGE YEAR
BY ALISTAIR HERBERT

SUN CREPT AROUND THE TALLER BUILDINGS in the middle distance, making the patchwork city look almost picturesque.

From her window in the government office Ivy could see street cleaners and vagrants milling around, colleagues hurrying in her direction across the square, fathers walking their children to the school buses, and leaves in the air. Autumn was coming. It was only a small corner of the city, but from this she extrapolated: in the far distance the old city walls crumbled under the weight of her namesake, and beyond the walls stretched canals and highways, farms and reservoirs, water-logged hills. Somewhere far north was the sea, the old church, her memory of her mother. She held it all inside her as she stood there, the hugeness of a world which would still be here tomorrow. It helped her identify from an impossible list of tasks the few things which were important enough to do today: brief the speakers, work on the bill, grant her replacement an interview, and try to find an hour with her legal counsel on the question of the unbreakable law.

Her career would end in twenty weeks. She had known before she took office that, on a fixed day, she would cede all right to govern, give up her home authority, and probably never usefully recover it, though she hadn't necessarily believed it. Even so, she'd grown up in the aftermath of the last change year, and the next would happen no matter what she did. The change law was inescapable.

The law was simple in wording and logically sound: equal rights were essential for all people, but the old world's war on inequality had pulled apart its society and failed to deliver a stable way of life. In the face of this paradox the government which formed after the last crisis had fixed in permanent statute a new law and a new way of organising the world: for twenty-five years commencing the day the new government took power, women would rule. Women formed the government, a woman was elected as first king, and women were to rule all households and industries. Men would be beholden to their mothers until they married, and owe only secondary allegiance to the state. When the twenty-five years came to a close, the terms would reverse and men would take the first place again in the order until their own twenty five years ended. If the change law was ever dismantled, the state would dissolve. It was the only truly permanent law and to touch it was necessarily to risk the end of the nation. It had been like this for one hundred and twenty-five years.

She was going to try to touch it.

Ivy knew the law as well as anyone, and she didn't dispute its usefulness. Every serious decision ultimately required a casting vote; delivering this efficiently required a leadership drawn from a small ruling class. Nevertheless, society no longer accepted hereditary inequality. The change law was far from perfect, but it worked. The problem was that it was getting in her way.

She had planned since infancy to take her own children north the same way her mother had taken her, initiate them in the old religion and perform the confirmation ceremony. Her parents had brought her up to honour traditional values, as trite as those words sounded in the modern era, when new laws came and went before people understood them, and new technologies came and went before laws could catch up to them. Lately the air itself felt charged with the idea of change —independent of the change year itself—and she was a part of it, but she still believed all the things she had grown up believing. It was written in her skin, her mother's refrain, her father echoing it behind her, and she not thinking to challenge something which seemed so obviously right, as right as the law: we do these things this way for a good reason, even if you can't see it. She would take her children north and hold the ceremony in the old church, and they would grow like her strong and happy in the world, grateful for everything it gave and to be a part of it, and ready for their own changes. It wouldn't be the same world she'd known, but the faith's exercises would help with that too. They would do a lot of good for two young girls who might struggle to find their place.

Except John didn't share her opinion, and in six months he would be in charge. They were good together, but they both knew where they differed, and he would stop her travelling north. He held her line when she said how things would be in the house—he even honoured her intentions when he explained things to their daughters, taking the time to explain how she felt about a question as well as what his own answer would be—but his private view was progressive. Ivy thought it was an inevitable consequence of his age: he was a year her junior and had known for all his young adulthood that his place was only temporary, that later a time would come when his power increased: burst into life from nothing, from a standing start, like the magic beans in the children's story. Or, for her, like the flash floods of her youth: one minute you're tending your garden in the valley the same way you've always done it, and the next you're digging through mud to see if anything survived. Of course they had different ideas. And he would oppose the ceremony—call it unscientific bunkum, a waste of time, an unwanted hangover from a less enlightened age. This was the same language of progress she used daily in her speeches.

She found it hard herself to cope with what was coming. She performed the church exercises daily in order to tend, alongside her leader's mind, a follower's mind which had never existed but which would take over in her life at the proper moment, which would bear witness to the leader she had been without letting that old self overpower the new necessary balance. She knew it was working: she could see the difference between her own bearing and that of her peers who didn't practice. In the power years it had been easy to say they didn't need these old rituals any more, these superstitions and folkways. But the closer the change loomed, the more she saw cracks appearing in the bullish veneer. Some of them would fall. Some always fell after change—and on both sides, because it wasn't just the leader's mind which struggled with its new role. The first years last time had been brutal, and their party had been working to make this time smoother: establish more rights, make things easier. Of course the change government could tear it all down, but the idea was that you made it easier on people now and they wouldn't bear so many grudges when they ended up in control. As change approaches, so ran her memorised line, we encourage our men to continue the good work we have done to support second-citizen interests.

If John wouldn't let her go north when her work was finished, the girls would never have their grandmother's gift. She had to find a way.

Laurel looked up warily as Ivy entered the legal counsel's office; the woman already had more than enough work. They were called counsels by tradition, but in this government the work hardly fit the title: they did everything, and Laurel would be working almost without rest until the final session of the outgoing government.

Ivy often told people that as an elected official she supported the law as often as she could manage it, and besides being a good joke it was also true: she did so vocally, from a position of power, because without doing so she would never get away with bending the rules as often as she did. It was the way things always worked, not just here but everywhere: the law was doing its job if things generally held together, whether or not any one law was actually obeyed. It didn't much matter whether the law in question was a petty by-law or a line from the constitution—Ivy knew that to run a country you sometimes had to ask the law to meet you halfway, and Laurel helped her make sure the law gave the right answer.

It was polite to begin with an apology—"I'm sorry to add to your burden, I hope you might give me your help," as the usual salutation went between women of office—but Ivy fell immediately into friendly informality. Laurel knew why she was here: they'd run this path together many times before. Protections of faith, gender assignment, inheritance to second-citizens, divorce law, even a look at protecting the status of former leaders who had held government posts. Laurel had worked through them all: summarised the proposal, mapped out intended and unintended consequences, checked interactions and conflicts with existing laws, estimated costs, and then carefully explained the reasons it wouldn't work. The last thing they'd looked at was making religious practice a legal right: everyone would have a right to perform the rituals of their faith regardless of the household leader's views. Laurel had worked patiently to convince her it wasn't going to happen. The state did not seek to govern the internal lives of its households or its citizens, and her new law would cause outcry about the dismantling of the sovereignty of the household. After the vote debates two years ago, where her party had sought to make votes anonymous so men could vote differently to their wives without reprisal, they couldn't afford another revival of that anger: it fed into the opposition party's hands right at the time of their only real chance to take power.

She'd been surprised at first by the response to the vote debate. Didn't they realise they would be the ones following household voting orders themselves in two elections' time? Were they so used to being in charge that they forgot things would change? But the public had been consistent and vehement in their response to the debate: the government needed to know its place. So since then she'd been searching for other options.

"I've come looking for a miracle," she said as she reached Laurel's desk. "I don't have a new idea, and I'm running out of time."

"Lucky for you," Laurel answered immediately, "I do. Not that you'll like it."

She listened as Laurel talked through the details, and why it was the only option left to them, and she tried to mask her scepticism until the older woman was finished explaining. A special leave of absence. She would gain permission to leave before the government dissolved, take the children north before the deadline, and do the ceremony then, before the year was out.

"It's early, I know—your daughters aren't properly of age—but it's better than nothing. And nothing's what they'll get if you wait."

Laurel was in her early forties and wore spectacles. She didn't look like the kind of person who made it this high in office; she had a hesitant frailty in her speech and walked slowly. Ivy suspected that this was an act—or, if it wasn't, that there was at least some other part of Laurel kept hidden from her which did the real work of fending off rivals and hiding the bodies. She still had no idea how the counsels' office organised its ranks.

"They'd just have to grow up fast," she answered, giving the proposal the fair chance it deserved. "But that's not the problem. The problem is the leave of absence itself."

Laurel smiled drily. "Ask your boss and see what she says. It's not strictly a legal question." She paused to let the joke sink in. "I'd almost like to see you ask her," she continued, "just to find out what would happen."

"Indeed. I'd need a reason she can't refuse. But there has to be something. Not a new law—we don't have time for that. Something already written."

Laurel sat back in her chair. This was why Ivy came to her: as busy as the woman was, she never really wanted to avoid the work. She didn't particularly care that Ivy's success would make her own life harder, because the puzzle itself was irresistible to her: the law's problems and contradictions, codes and delicacies, were alive to her, and coming to her with a legal problem was like putting a nail in front of a hammer.

"Bereavement wouldn't do it," Laurel said as she came out of her thinking. "Even if you had any bereavements you wanted to suffer. Hospitalisation might, but you'd have to be so hurt you wouldn't be able to travel—and besides, they'd probably bring work to your bedside, at least for authorisation. A scandal might get you dismissed, but also locked up. Not that it's easy to arrange a scandal nowadays anyway." She sniffed. "I can look, but I'm not sure what else I'll find. Unless you have something to use to blackmail her."

Ivy smiled again. They both knew their boss was untouchable. She was as pure as the constitution itself. When the change finally came and it was time for her to step down, Ivy half expected her to turn into steam and disappear forever.

"Royal dispensation still happens," she offered, but Laurel shook her head.

"Pardons for criminals and honours for heroes, yes, but you're neither. You're stuck in the middle with the rest of us. You have to play by the rules."

"Or if I was unfit for duty? If I was a danger to the work?"

Laurel's head tilted. "Like how?" Ivy chose her words carefully.

"What if," she started, "what if I felt certain that keeping me here would do more harm than good for some reason. If, say, I had a mental breakdown, or a crisis, in private, with her, and she thought if I stayed in my office any longer I'd fall apart in public and destroy her programme. Implode and take her with me. Too volatile. Better to retire me than risk it."

Laurel gave her a long look. A strand of her hair had come loose and would stay loose until she could wash her hands. "Your career would be finished for a start."

She shrugged. "That's true of us both, soon enough."

"That's not the same. I'll be alright after, and you will too if you do your job. If you try something like this—well, who knows. And how will you like living under a husband who knows you destroyed his family's reputation before he even had chance to use it?"

"John's a good man," Ivy answered after a pause. "He'll understand." Laurel nodded.

"And your legacy?"

She had placed her pen carefully on the desk and was resting her chin on linked hands. The black marks of the scribe coloured her hands' edges: the ink stained everything it touched. When Laurel became a housewife—she had a husband out near the city wall whom Laurel had never met—the smudges would fade slowly over months as new skin replaced them, and new jobs took the ink's place.

She thought about the question, but not for long enough to untangle her thoughts. She did have a legacy. She had risen rapidly in government and was the youngest top level representative in the new state's history—if not for the surprise of a second child, she might have gone even further. She had done good work. Now she was leaving it for something unknown. She was accustomed to winning, but what did winning look like, in this game? "It doesn't change anything," she answered, too quickly. She needed to be decisive or Laurel would doubt her. "My girls are my legacy now," she added more certainly. "I'm ready for the change. I'm ready for my future. That's why I need this: to pass on my acceptance to my children, to pass on my faith. You know that."

Laurel looked sceptical. But she always looked sceptical.

"All very well for yourself," she said when she was done thinking about it. "And the work? I have seven bills from you alone for the next session—bills you actually bullied me into working on because you said they were the difference between life and death for all of us. Crucial to post-change womanhood, I think you said."

Ivy was still standing; she sat at work only when it seemed impossible to refuse the invitation. Never relax in the company of enemies, her mother had instructed, and there were always enemies here, but now she took the seat she had previously ignored. This is what John will find hardest to learn, she thought: the change from being one person to being many, all existing alongside each other with different duties. How do you choose between one duty and another, between all these things you must do as your different people? It's silly to claim that there is one you who must take precedence. They're all you. So where does your allegiance belong?

"It's not an easy choice to make," she said at last, and Laurel shook her head.

"Every choice is made instantly, it's just living with some them that's hard. You don't like this choice because you don't want to live with the choice you know you ought to make."

She felt foolish talking like this in the halls of office. The last month, some of her colleagues were calling it, as if the world would end when they stepped down. Not for her. Not for them.

"I've taken up too much of your time," she said, excusing herself. "Thank you. Look into it. Write me a page or two on outcomes, nothing detailed. I'll give it a week to decide."

Outside it was cold and the sky showed stars. She trusted Laurel—she trusted everyone she led. If you don't trust them, they're not yours to lead. The secret was safe until she chose whether or not to deploy it.

Another week had ended. Nineteen to go.

At home they were helping the maid with the laundry, a task which felt impossible alone but trivially easy when shared by a team of four. When it was done the maid took the pot from the oven and then her leave, returning home to her own husband's care and company and leaving John to serve his family's meal. The maid, she knew, was a sign of their fortune. Inequality here was still a real thing; solving the problem at a state level had made the state viable, had restored the family household to its rightful place at the heart of human life, but there were still big houses and small houses, and people still went hungry. In the restaurants, so she heard from her colleagues, the younger women argued with their older peers about who was worse off because of the coming changes: the ones still in apprenticeship who could change their paths and seek out husbands and easy work now, before the new year, or the ones who had to wait and might find nothing, but who at least had experienced serious work for a time. Some of them would be much poorer after the change, and for the most part they viewed their futures with grim realism.

Ivy was one of them, but she heard their arguments second hand at her desk, as she had little enough time with her family without visiting restaurants. She had married as early as possible, become pregnant as early as permitted, wanted her child to know the world before it changed because she loved her world so much herself. And she had known her plan for her own adulthood—had pursued it ruthlessly, knowing her time was limited—and in balance to this she had promised herself always to owe her children her time as much as she owed it to anyone.

They ate and listened to the girls' stories of adventures, and when the girls went to bathe they let them go alone, old enough now to be trusted with the water, and she and John sat and made conversation about the day's news. She wanted to hear what he thought about the transition debates, what had filtered out to the radio news and how he interpreted it. He spun it out for her with that skill he had for seeing through the bluster and for guessing her colleagues' real motivations. He was uncannily astute—he always knew before her which politicians were taking bribes, just by listening to the news broadcasts—and as he talked she watched his face, his thinking, and she fancied she could see the reason they understood government so differently. His was the interest of the outsider, a spectator at a sports game, analysing form and predicting for the fun of it, where she was on the field and looking for her real opportunities. He had the clearer view of the visible action but no access to the secrets, and he had to guess at them where she often knew.

"Of course," he said lightly, "if we had real equality this debate wouldn't be necessary."

"We can't afford real equality," she replied, knowing that again she was playing the role he had given her in their discussions, the villain's place she had accepted. She knew that if he couldn't be in control of his own life then he needed at least to be right about things, to be on the side of righteousness, and so in their life of two minds she would need to play the cynical realist as his foil. "We never could afford real equality. We saw the contradiction and couldn't solve it, it's all there in the constitution. We have to work with what we've got."

"I wonder," he said as he reached to take her plate, "if you'll still believe that when you're the one washing up."

She let him win—she had to let him win—and went to put the girls to bed. They followed happily as she called them from the bath, towels trailing and skin still wet. She scolded them, warned them they'd catch cold, and they didn't care, tired and relaxed in that way she often saw but still only understood as an outsider, the tiredness which followed long days with a father who loved them. She sat between them in bed and they read together, and she thought about the magic beans, the giant's house, the axe which brought it down. The golden goose who would lay for any master. Then while they lay down and drifted closer to sleep, talking to each other quietly across the space between their beds, she stood in the hallway and performed the exercises. The practice.

"Mum?" Hazel's voice. She paused in her work.

"Yes?"

"Will you be a different person, after the change year?"

She moved to the doorway. "How do you mean?"

"I mean will you still do the same things with us?"

She sat down. "Well, that's why I do these exercises. Because it will be a big change, and I need to be strong to meet it. I don't think I will still do the same things with you, your father and I will both do different things, but we'll both still be here. You remember when you were little and you didn't go to school? And when you're big you won't again. We've all changed before and we can do it again." She spoke softly and slowly, the same voice she used to read stories.

"Mum?" This time it was Holly. Strange how often they took over each other's thoughts and conversations, and both let it happen. Holly was small, smaller than she should be for her age but she ran with the other children all the same and hated to be singled out. She liked to be hugged more than Hazel, who was more likely to endure a cuddle from her mother than go looking for one.

"Yes, my love?"

"Will we do the exercises too? So we can be strong to meet it?"

She touched her daughter's head. The candle's flicker put half the girl's face in shadow, but she knew the shape of the features by heart.

"Do you know," she said quietly, scared to break the room's stillness, "I honestly don't know. Your father and I see things differently, and he will be leader soon." She broke off. "Do you know," she began again, "why I gave you your names?" This was a story they knew. This was the better story to tell while they drifted to sleep. "I named you Hazel, for Hazel's flexibility. I knew you would need to be flexible. Hazel grows in many shapes and stands up to hard times, and it bends in the wind and lives and makes beautiful things. That's how I thought on your naming day. And I named you Holly because Holly can grow tall or grow small, and can grow sharp leaves or soft leaves. Holly grows its sharp teeth only when predators come to feed on it. We had no deer near the city for a hundred years, did you know that? But the Holly remembered and when the deer came back the Holly grew sharp leaves again. I named you Holly so that, if you get bitten, you'll bite back. Do you remember how people change all the time? Well that's two different people I have been."

Hazel yawned. "I want to learn the exercises."

"You can only learn the exercises when you've been confirmed. That's how it works."

"I want to be confirmed." Another yawn. Almost asleep. Almost there. It was like magic, watching it happen. She could not feel tired while she watched this happening.

"We all want things, my love. You're only eleven."

"Can't eleven-year-olds get confirmed?"

She paused. "Maybe. We'll see."

"What about eight-year-olds?" Holly wasn't as drowsy as her sister, she was fighting off sleep, starting to sit up again in her bed, interested and not willing to be left out. Ivy eased her down again onto her back and she fought to roll over and get comfortable, huffing into her pillow.

"Maybe," she said again. "Just because something never happened before, that doesn't mean it can never happen. It all depends." She stood to leave, her feet cold on the bare floor, and saw for a moment her own mother in her place.

What do you want most? her own mother had asked her, when she found out she was pregnant again, the timing all wrong against her careful plan, and she hadn't known what to do. You don't get everything you want in life. You have to be lucky to get even one thing. So which one thing do you want most? The big job or the child? It was the last time she visited the north coast: no later opportunity had presented itself. Her mother's hair had been thin and white, almost translucent where it lifted from her head, strange to see. I want the child, she said, and her mother held her and told her: Then be happy. Live the life that you want. Yes, she thought now in the bedroom, she wanted the child. They could have thrown her out of office, they could have put her on the street, they could have pretended her work never happened, and she still would have chosen the child.

"Mum?"

She paused again. "Yes?"

"What does it depend on?"

She turned back and pressed the cover down, fixing it around her daughter's shape. "Enough questions for one night." And she blew out the candle and left them to drift away.

On the stairs she paused, not quite ready to face her husband, because she didn't know quite what she wanted to say. Politics had taught her deceit but it didn't come easily at home: she wanted to tell him her thoughts but she knew that she couldn't—not until it was decided. The debate would only confuse her motives and her feelings. She already knew what he thought, and as leader she must keep her doubts to herself, because an uncertain leader was not a leader. Her mother taught her this, too, though she had never ruled anything herself, barely even pretending to instruct her husband in the years of Ivy's childhood. She had taken her daughter north at his bidding, and avoided the call for leaders, though she came from good stock, and poured her life into Ivy. She trained her not to be a particular thing but rather to choose one thing for herself and pursue it with ferocity—and to choose well. We get so caught up in the politics, she had said when Ivy asked why she left the city, when Ivy had already decided to go back and serve, that we forget about the real business of living. Don't do that. She made no attempt to stop her going.

She watched him finish washing dishes, then linked her arms around him from behind and got in his way as he tried to put things in cupboards. In the end he gave up and came to sit with her on the good chair, and they talked about—

what else?—politics. He thought her last welfare bill didn't go far enough, that she should have pushed it further to better protect against backlash in the months following change day: there would be a lot of single women looking for secure work, and not all of them would find it. Ivy thought she'd already gone too far with the bill in question: they'd made provisions which would be too expensive to maintain—money might grow on trees, but housing didn't—and it would be repealed by the incoming government.

She didn't much mind, because it wasn't the welfare bill on which she was staking her success. Hidden behind it, not that he knew, was a minor amendment to workhouse regulations which would place fixed quantity quotas on handmade goods, which she had sold as a cheap way to meet clean energy goals but was really designed to force the houses out of machine labour entirely: when the timber bubble burst, as it would quite soon, they would have to convert all production to handmade as the only way to meet the fixed quota without overproducing. Her hope was that, by the time they got anywhere near to amending the law to stipulate percentage quotas instead of fixed quantities, someone might have recognised that employing actual people actually worked.

It was the only way anything ever really changed; it was what made Laurel, a mere legal counsel, her most powerful ally. Even in power, she had learned, you couldn't just tell them what you wanted, because they'd give you half of it. You had to make it happen before anyone noticed, pretend it was a happy accident, then manage the fallout. She knew plenty of her peers were capable of playing the same game—some of them much better than her—and a large part of the interest after the change year would be seeing the secret consequences of other people's bills, being able to trace them back and see what had really driven each piece of legislation.

"It'll be interesting," John said, no telling how his thoughts had led him from this to that to this, "to see how quickly they fix whatever's been getting in the way for the last twenty years."

She frowned. "What do you mean?"

"Well I mean, you know, how all this time nothing's changed. I wonder how long it will take before we start making real progress."

"Real progress." She repeated his words, not trying to make a point, only to feel the shape of them in her mouth. Understand what they meant.

"You know. I mean, I know it's all kept ticking over and I know how hard you all work to keep things steady, but what have we really achieved? Not anywhere near as much as we should have done."

What have we achieved? It wasn't a posture, she realised. It wasn't a trick. He wasn't teasing her. This was the shape of his world, as fixed as her own but contorted, a wrong shape. Her government was a failure and it was well past time for someone else to take a turn. He meant it and didn't even intend for his words to hurt her: it was just what he believed. It was what they all believed, for all she knew.

She thought about the trade crisis six years ago. The knock on effects from that which almost brought the mines to a standstill for want of a component the size of a fingernail. The falling bridge two summers ago which trapped grain out at the farms while the city hungered. The time their neighbours to the north closed the borders and they had to send soldiers in the night to gather intelligence. A thousand similar things. And then, on top of whatever was happening in the real world, the endless dramas of personality and ego and ambition which made it impossible to do anything out in the open lest your colleagues throw you to the wolves to serve their own goals. All the times the coalition at the top of the party had almost fallen apart, and she'd been home late and telling the girls sorry, I'm sorry, there was something important at work, and the important thing had been another all-night council where they ran over the same disputes as the last time. The impossibility of it all. The country stretching south, east, west, river and ocean and waste and farm. Three different languages and they thought the government would hold them together while they fought in the street. The slow death of every empire. Delicately managing all this was—had been—her life's work.

"We achieved," she answered, her hand no longer touching him, "what you sit down to eat every night. Food on our table and living daughters. Laws which work. Roofs and shoes and news to keep people busy while they argue at dinnertime. More people with jobs than not. The survival of a nation state for a quarter of a century. If the next court achieves the same, I will count our lives blessed."

She stood from the chair and faced him square, wanting acknowledgement. He was looking away from her, across into the fire. This was it, she realised: twice she had rebuked him before, only twice in a marriage of twelve years, and this was the last time she would ever do it. The next time this happened, it would be her with the lowered eyes. She stood in silence and at last he looked up and they stood that way for a time, then he nodded his respect, lowered his eyes again, and stood to take his leave. She watched him as he walked to the sink and resumed putting dishes in cupboards, and she stood still until she decided what to do. It came so easily, this tyranny. To shut it off would be a life's work, and success was not guaranteed. She had seen them, the middle aged men in the street who had failed to adapt. She didn't delude herself that she was so much better than them.

What does it depend on, the girls had asked her, and the question was about more than just the exercises. The ceremony. The government. The transition. The onward limp of the nation. The patchwork city. The survival of her own household, before and after the change. Herself as leader and follower: two selves in one house, as the ceremony said. The happiness of her daughters, Holly and Hazel, who would never be what she had been.

Me, she thought, watching her husband clatter plates grumpily, ignorant of her deepest concerns. It depends on me. And she realised she had already made her decision.

Following the Crows

by Violet Bertelsen

CHRIST OF THE OAKS IS NO STRANGER TO THE ENTANGLEMENTS OF LOVE. Luckily for us, Christ doesn't usually try to seduce mortals, as his wife Death is very jealous. They share a bed by the water where fast water becomes slow and the irises grows. She clings to the shoreline; she is the shore.

Death once lived in the willow tree, but Christ convinced her to move to the shore by the irises, so humans could make baskets of the willow branches. After Death moved from the willow, the little people moved in and they caused no end of problems with those who dared to harvest the willow branch. Christ then pleaded— and there are many, many colorful tales of the lengths he was forced to go—to get the little people to leave the willow so it could be safe for people to take. Technically the arrangement is that the willow is on loan to Christ from Death. But then again, legally speaking at least, everything is leased from Death.

Christ is also lovers with Little Deer, who lives in the tulip tree. Little Deer is a beloved goddess. She has golden fur and little antlers, cloven hooves, human hands and the tail of a white-tailed deer. Her face is unspeakably beautiful.

Upon making the rank, the sign of the Elder bush is tattooed on the top of the right foot of journeymen Herbalists. There are other tattoos as well that signify standing in society; peasants all have the sign of the apple tree and another that signifies clan allegiance. The majority of peasants belong both to apple clan and worship the God of the Harvest, and have apples tattooed on both feet. These poor souls are, good-naturedly or not, the butt of many jokes. Other families are devotees of the hawthorn and have the gift of song. Some are jolly and cunning and their foot shows the four leaf and acorn pattern of Christ. Especially beautiful people are born with the mark of Little Deer and are legendary for marrying up; Little Deer is irresistible.

Those born into the crafting clans wear the mark of the willow, but exceptional artists have the willow tattoo transformed deftly into the mark of the tulip tree. Anyone who creates beauty is associated with Little Deer, since she is such a lover of beauty. Professional prostitutes wear the mark of the pine on the right foot and the tulip tree on the left. With professional soldiers this is reversed.

Of course, sometimes people are born into something and then step into another, which is why often only one foot is tattooed at twenty years and the other may be free until immediately before death.

We believe that it is important to respectfully laugh at the gods and to thus keep them from utterly possessing us. Or at least laugh with them. It isn't prudent though to laugh at the Virgin of the Maples who blushes crimson and will sometimes swoon, crushing sod houses in her wake.

The highest mark is the hexagon, and is worn on the left hand by royalty and on the right hand by beekeepers.

Our houses are cut like honey combs into the Knoll. On top we plant thyme. Rabbits will line their warrens with thyme if they are able to, and the rabbits are our teachers. By the little overhanging stone-arch window vents, families will often plant lemon balm to bring the bees and sweeten the smell of their little earthen hexagon.

Our saints plant trees, and Esperanza is the greatest saint in living memory. Later I would hear tales of her exploits, the very wanderings that fill my memory: Esperanza and I would transplant cuttings, rake in seeds, and caress each other to the point of delirium. Then we wandered aimlessly for dozens of miles to gather seeds in their season. During winter we would lodge in the closest town, wherever that may be, and do healing work and odd jobs until early spring when we'd set out again with our rake and shovels and baskets of seeds we carried in relay.

Little Deer teaches the arts of love. The ancients had forgotten the arts of love, and this displeased Little Deer. She sent out horrific plagues of chronic sickness in the bellies of ticks who rode upon deer like cavalrymen on horses. She was disgusted that humans no longer touched one another and instead would give rough handshakes and artlessly engage in a few minutes of hasty unpleasant coitus before falling asleep. So she loosed this plague to force those without touch to finally receive caress. Still, many couldn't and they died in agony. With time, some great prostitutes, high priestesses of love, were able to finally hear Little Deer in their hearts and taught people the secrets of caress. After this, Little Deer was grateful to have been heard, and forever protected the prostitutes and and granted them her mysteries of healing.

Now, every two-apple peasant knows that love is the art of caress and that the orgasm is simply a particularly demanding aspect of caress. Not everyone is skilled at orgasm; women tend to be less skilled than men, but are typically better at the subtle canvas of touch. For those knowledgeable in these ways of Little Deer, there is much technical language concerning the art of love. Sadly, I am ignorant in this; I am trained in the art of the forest and the cures of the body—that is, the Healer arts of the Elder bush by the shore. Esperanza was a prostitute before Christ revealed himself to her in an oak tree and bade her to plant his seeds, and the seeds of all trees. Prior to this, she had been a passionate devotee of Little Deer. During our time together, she focused intently on her commitments to Christ. Of course, while we made love we were devotional to Little Deer and we explored her mysteries.

Thieves and murderers walk the same desolate countryside that saints do. As such our Christ answers to both types: thieves and saints. We wear our robes of green and the thieves leave us be. At times they even bring provisions: a chicken stolen from a peasant, a basket of apples, fresh wheat bread. Other times they become drunk on the power of Christ and help us plant trees.

Esperanza laughed easily. Her favorite food was garlic. "The most favored food of all great prostitutes," she told me. She could size up a man in a single glance and then have her way with him. She extended her powers even to Christ himself. She related how she told Christ, "Lord, thank you for what you do for me and, with all my heart, I am forever grateful. But you must understand, I do this not for you, but for the trees," and Christ laughed his merry laugh that sends electricity up and down your spine like a thousand orgasms.

Christ favored Esperanza's spunk. He wouldn't trust you unless he could see the dirt on your hands.

When I met Esperanza she was experimenting with transplanting little oaks to see if that might be a better method than hauling the heavy acorns, though she eventually had to abandon the project. I was gathering food in the woods that summer when I saw her. I was twenty, I remember, and had just received the Elder bush tattoo of the journeyman herbalist. While approaching, I noticed there was a murder of crows in a nearby oak tree watching her silently. Below them she was examining very closely the taproots of the baby oaks, praying under her breath, and she seemed to carry an immense silence that immediately attracted me. Never before or since have I felt silence as profound as when I was with her. Not sure whether to slip away or to approach, I stood motionless watching her. She stopped, raised her eyes, and took me in for a very long moment as the silence rose and fell like great waves. There was a little half smile on her face and then out of nowhere she laughed sweetly. "Hello. I call myself Esperanza. What is your name?"

"Poquitas Montañas," I replied, trying not to blush or smile and failing to stop either. "May I ask you what you may be doing in our forests?" I continued, now blushing hotly all over.

She again gave her strange half smile, which suggested utter confidence, and again I felt the pulse of her silence run through my body. "I plant trees," she responded simply. "You may help me."

Without a moment's hesitation, I dropped the basket I was collecting mushrooms in and began helping her dig up little oak trees. We carried them six miles to a hillside and planted them, carefully watering them in with willow water.

"It helps the roots," she explained. The sun was setting and we hastily made a fire. She hung a tarp and mosquito netting while I cooked the mushrooms in a cast iron pan with garlic. "You may sleep in the mosquito netting with me, Poquitas Montañas," she said, and I nodded. "You may enter." Again I nodded. She struck a match to a thick marijuana cigarette and we smoked it to ashes and then I let her seduce me.

Later, she confessed she had been going out of her mind with loneliness before I began to sleep in her tent, that I saved her from madness. She was an excellent lover, and never once did I resent how cleverly she ensnared my heart and procured a sidekick in the bargain.

She often said "Pleasure is the greatest art." Even while we starved and scratched out a living eating insects and the cambium of saplings and even river mud, she made our time together the best of my entire life through the arts of Little Deer. Never once did she forget to compliment my cooking. It was always my job to prepare food, to forage and set the snares. Many times she mentioned the terrible hunger that had afflicted her for years and how Christ himself had to intervene many times and make his acorns sweet for her or else she would have perished. "Times were hard before you came and joined me, Poquitas Montañas," she'd sigh after a meal of cattail leaves and grubs.

One day I could no longer contain my curiosity. "Why do you do this?" I asked her.

"Do what?" she replied, her eyes half closed, emanating an immense and sensual silence.

"Why do you wander around endlessly planting trees? You've faced years of starvation when you are still beautiful and skilled in the art of love and could easily return to a life of ease and pleasure and much respect," I said, feeling increasingly confused as she showed more of her teeth in her enormous smile.

"There is a simple answer to that and a not so simple answer and I will answer as truthfully as possible. It is clear that you love me sincerely, and so it would be a very great sin to cross your heart with lies. The simple reason is that Christ of the Oaks came to me and told me to plant trees. The more honest answer is that before Christ came I was lost and drowning in life and he saved me. Oh, Poquitas Montañas! I was terribly sad, desperately sad in my old life. There are many ways I can explain that sadness. It was the sadness that everyone feels being alive, but I was sick on it. It is a terrible power to be able to manipulate people to the degree I can, and to get more silver to manipulate the right person correctly than a two-apple peasant sees in a lifetime. I did a good job, but when I was alone I could see that I was cruel and petty and selfish, and even evil. I couldn't control all of me, and so I lived in fear of the unruly parts of myself. I prayed fervently to all the gods and Christ looked me into the eyes and said, 'You are asking the wrong sorts of questions. That is your problem. Why not just go out and plant trees?' And with those words he conquered my heart. He sent his crows to lead me and they led me hither and thither and then to you." She paused and gave me a sly look. "And then I could ask you why you dropped everything and came to follow me?"

"In all honesty, I fell in love and had nothing better to do," I said, confused again.

"Yes, precisely," she said with her half smile.

We had this conversation immediately before she began to take sick, although we didn't then know that she only had a half a year to live. She began having a nasty little cough that wouldn't go away, no matter what herbs I gave her.

While we worked under the disinterested eyes of crows, we talked greedily about every subject under the sun, and even some that reside below the earth. She taught me about the ancients.

"The ancients were great counters," said Esperanza. "They could command numbers to do as they pleased. They counted each seed of a tree, and found that each tree in its lifetime was only able to establish one seed for the future forest. One out of uncountable millions. But we, through gathering the seeds and carefully planting them, can make thousands of the seeds grow. This is consecration, and redemption is one of the Mysteries of Christ."

She explained later, though, that the ancients with their fevered numbers tended to die badly and become ghosts. "People die for different reasons: some people die in war, others die of broken hearts, and still others die from being spurned. Others die simply from hunger or a sickness. Ghosts, though, are easy to dispel. Let them talk into your heart but say no words yourself, give them nothing to hold onto, and give them a flower of the iris. If they take it, then they are ready to truly die. If they don't you can simply banish them."

One time in particular stands out in my memory. Following the crows, we entered a glade that seemed a little darker than it should have. There was a dark malign presence and she mouthed the word *ghost* to me.

She approached the point that rent the glade into darkness. For a long while she listened and nodded her head and said nothing. Then we went to a stream bank and found some irises growing right where fast water slowed down. She put the flower on a rock and the space brightened, and then we drank from a spring and made love on the moss.

Long ago the ancients made poisons that hurt the beautiful earth. With malicious glee, with a mind fevered with hot screaming numbers, they spread invisible poisons. Now the poisons can only be observed indirectly, by absence. In moderately poisoned areas there are no hawks or frogs, and evil spirits attack and draw blood from wary travelers who sleep unprotected by a ring of yarrow. In very bad places there is hardly life at all, and the spirits snarl and bite at dark like maddened dogs. For this reason, we carry a basket of ailanthus seed. In these places of desolation, it alone will thrive and send up trunks twenty meters tall. "When the trees return, the spirits are tamed," explained Esperanza as we walked quickly, leaving a dead zone and following the crows as the sun set. And so we loved the ailanthus and listened carefully to hear him, but he is a trickster who infests gardens and said nothing to us except exuberant nonsense.

Because of these ancient poisons most people succumb to cancer in their forties, if something else doesn't kill them first. Esperanza was thirty-four and she was dying. At first she had only a cough and a sore throat. Slowly she began to lose her ability to eat, and then to breathe. Trying to heal her, I looked in her throat and saw that she was being corroded by cancer. She bore the mark of Death, and so it would be an impropriety against the goddess for me to do more trying to heal her.

The crows led us into a village where the great basket festivity was taking place. The locals were taking baskets filled with everything they wanted to release from their lives to a great fire in the center of the town, where all the spent marijuana scraps of the season burned to bring forgetfulness. Everyone was deliciously stoned, dancing, playing musical instruments and feasting. Esperanza struggled for every breath and then was racked by pained, coughing laughter at the absurdity of the situation. She clutched me with her boney hands and whispered in my ear, "For that he rises." Then she died, and the crows which had been watching from the eaves of houses flew up and, circling overhead three times, disappeared, never to return.

Winter was coming. The townsfolk helped me dig a grave on the outskirts of town and I planted a white oak tree on top. Altogether, Esperanza had been a saint for fourteen years. I had been with her only for the last two and a half of that time.

With nothing better to do, and nowhere to go, I settled in the village where Esperanza died and scratched out a living gardening, foraging, and trading my healing work. An apple and willow family partitioned a corner of their earthen hexagon for sleeping space. They shared their meager food for me simple-heartedly. This was a poor town, where no silver flowed and everyone shared their surplus and together managed to make do. My first winter there I was so overwhelmed by generosity that I realized, with a certain pang of sadness, that my debt was too great for me to ever leave responsibly. This must have pleased the Abuelas who presided over the town; they made it clear that they liked me and were eager to marry their grandsons to me. Several years later, when I took Tila, a younger woman apprenticing in herb craft, as my lover, they simply switched to imploring my hand ironically.

After many years, Tila reached a certain level of proficiency at herb craft and the arts of healing. Then, I finally manage to feel okay leaving the village for a few weeks. I left her there as a sort of guarantee of my return and ventured off to see how the trees Esperanza and I planted had grown.

About a days walk from the village I came to what had been a vast dead zone, that was now overrun by ailanthuses five meters tall. There was a silence there in between the rustling of the leaves that reminded me of Esperanza, but it wasn't sinister like a ghost, it was warm and kind, not needy and grasping. Insects abounded and there were even small birds.

Further out the maples had grown stout and were about as tall as I was, the oaks half a meter. The tulip trees were too tall for me to touch their top leaf and rustled with the clove hoofed preciousness of Little Deer.

Amongst the little oaks I saw a murder of crows in the little branches watching me, and I knew that if I prayed to Christ he would grant me safe passage to take up his calling to plant more trees.

Much sooner than I expected I returned home, thoroughly satisfied with what I had seen. At some point, if I lived long enough, I imagined I would return to the life of a saint. I could wait, though; I wasn't as tormented as Esperanza.

Later that night, while caressing with Tila, she asked me, with her nails softly scratching my arm and back, "Do you ever think of returning to the forests and planting more?"

"Someday," I said playfully, running my fingers through her hair and then touching each of her vertebrate as if counting. "Someday."

HURRY UP AND WAIT

BY HOLLY SCHOFIELD

I DUG MY LEFT TOE FARTHER INTO THE LOOSE DIRT OF THE CLIFF and gripped a scraggly salal bush. The cell phone had landed on an outcrop a full meter away, beyond a patch of tall, yellowing grass. Western fescue. Slippery stuff, this late in the year. My right foot dangled above a large rock, slick with Oregon moss. A seagull shrieked far below, wheeling over the ocean. *Don't look down.* I eased onto the inner edge of the rock, shifting my weight off my aching left leg.

The rock overbalanced. I jerked back and listened to it crash against garry oak and scrubby arbutus as it fell and fell and fell. No splash—the tide was out.

"Mike! Have you got it yet?" Darren's voice drifted down the tattered edge of Lovat's Bluff far above me. Trust a salesman to say my name when there were only the two of us on the island.

The wind tugged at my shirt and dead leaves whirled past me, then were whisked away toward Alaska, several hundred kilometers to the north. I carefully put my foot in the divot the rock had left behind, and stretched across the grassy vertical slope, pretending I was thirty years old, not sixty. I snagged the cell phone and shoved it in my jeans.

My arm muscles were trembling with fatigue by the time I hauled myself over the top of the cliff. I gripped a near-horizontal arbutus bole and staggered to my feet before handing Darren the phone. He danced around me, his filthy dress shirt neatly tucked into his pinstriped pants and his hair smoothed in place, chattering away—something about the phone and the photos on it.

He made the phone play a little song of some kind, tinny and false compared to the chatter of the kinglets rummaging for insects in the forest litter. Their yellow-striped heads flashed occasionally, adding color to the green-on-brown Gulf Island palette.

I tuned him out and looked out over the ocean. A few small islands, green hummocks dotting the grey white-capped sea, then nothing—all the way to Japan. I'd bought my little bit of paradise three decades ago: a cabin and five acres of second -growth Douglas fir—just prior to the remainder of the island being legislated as a provincial park. Long before everything went to hell. Sometimes, I felt I'd been preparing for this my whole life.

Darren was still caressing the phone's buttons like he was stroking a rosary. I held up a hand when he started a third thank you. I'd only retrieved the phone because he wouldn't shut up about it.

He looked sheepish. "Mike, you know I would have tried to go down the cliff myself."

"Sure, kid, you could have—before."

Darren still had fluid in his lungs and some muscle loss. The supernovovirus had hit him hard and there had been days when I thought he wasn't going to make it. I didn't think most Canadians had. Probably. Or Americans. Maybe. The whole world might be gone. Possibly. All I knew is a month ago, when CBC radio had gone silent and Air Canada stopped leaving contrails overhead, things must have gotten bad out there.

Just my luck. To be alone on a tiny island with a scrawny ex-insurance agent who couldn't tell blackberry from skunk cabbage, didn't know how to cut wood, and valued that stupid thing called social interaction.

I slapped down my cards. "Gin."

"No, it isn't." Darren snapped out of his reverie and studied my hand. "Cheater."

"Just wanting to see if you were paying attention." I smiled a thin smile, the only kind I knew how to do these days, and stretched my legs out under the kitchen table. Darren scooted his chair back a bit and put his feet on the chair rungs. He knew he crowded up my cabin.

I'd gradually been turning the cedar-sided bungalow into my retirement home, every holiday I could spare from my plumbing business in Vancouver. From where I sat at the birch table it had taken me a full year of weekends to make, I could feel the heat radiating from my nicely restored Selkirk woodstove. It squatted in the middle of the west wall, framed by two big curtainless windows overlooking the cove. A fir-plank coffee table and a very comfortable sofa, where Darren now slept, faced the stove's glass door. Behind me a small galley-style kitchen, now almost useless without propane, opened out to a wood porch. A short hallway led to my bedroom, my sanctuary from Darren.

"You know I ain't much for card games. We could be reading something if you charged a couple of batteries for the LED lamps instead of your phone." Darren's palm-sized solar-powered phone charger had been a Christmas gag gift from his girlfriend who had felt he spent far too much time on social media. She'd put it in his briefcase when he'd left that day: the day his plane had gone down in the storm. She'd been in Toronto when the bombs hit. He never mentioned her to me after that first time but sometimes I heard him sobbing in the night.

"Maybe we could capture the methane in the outhouse and use it to run the generator so we could try the radio?"

"Yeah, good idea, Darren. And then we could MacGyver the old log splitter into a submarine and go south to Mexico."

"Hey, be nice to me. I'm pretty vulnerable right now." He rubbed his forehead and snuffled a bit.

The fire was almost coals again. I got up and added some rather green fir, putting a handful of paper in just to give it a boost. I glanced at it before I crumpled it, some kind of confidentiality agreement from Darren's file folders. He'd consented to burning his papers after I made him collect twigs for three hours steady last week. The rain spattered on the south window and a sudden huge gust of wind made smoke billow out just as I closed the woodstove door. The weather was growing more and more unpredictable. Maybe because of the quake, or the European bombings, or the slow ebb and flow of climate change. I'd given up trying to list all the events that had led up to the world going silent—a sort of "perfect storm" that Darren had named "The Wipe."

"Mike, what *were* you going to do all day, living here, if things had worked out?" Darren bit his lip and leaned forward. "I really want to know."

"It would have been peachy keen, buddy, peachy keen. No throngs of irritating whiners, no lowlifes, no waiting in line at the grocery store, no mowing a lawn. Civilization sucks. It would have been heaven."

"Would have been?" Darren pounced on the words. "So it won't be heaven, being here with me, after the world's been Wiped? Which am I, an irritating whiner or a lowlife?" His sensitivity over his career choice was amazing. I almost smiled.

What *did* I want? *Could* I make it here, post-Wipe? I fiddled with the deck of cards. Eventually, there would be no white sugar, no flour, no milk powder. What would I do when the soda crackers ran out? Why hadn't I worked a bit harder, earlier, faster, to make this place self-sufficient? A dozen things needed to be done, but without tools and basic supplies and, most importantly, without *power*, they would be almost impossible. I'd had twenty solar panels, an inverter, and AGM batteries all on order from a Vancouver supplier. I'd planned to pick them up five weeks ago, right when the quarantines were announced. A week or so before the huge storm that had ripped both of my boats off their moorings and had blown Darren's seaplane off course.

"What you don't realize, old man, is that what you do affects the people around you. Your actions ripple outwards, like throwing a stone in a pond."

I'd had enough. The solitude of my bedroom would feel good. Darren's cell phone chimed as I crossed the tiny living room. He grabbed it. "Oh, right, a reminder to sew up the holes in my pants."

The phone beeped again, a different tone, more of a trill.

"Reminding you it's time to clean your toenails?" I jeered, from the doorway.

"It's an incoming text," Darren said in a funny voice and he bit his lip again. He sat down, rocking his chair a bit.

"You're shitting me." I tried to peer at the tiny screen but couldn't see a thing from across the room. The cell phone towers had lasted a couple of days after the commercial radio stations had died, during my final weekend visit here. My land line had died a week or so after that. I'd spent a full day phoning every number I knew and listening to silence or endless, unanswered ringing.

Darren's sweat smelled raw and new. This was for real.

"I've got half a bar of signal. And a text message," Darren said. He gently tapped the screen.

"ANYONE OUT THERE? TEXT BACK AT DUSK EACH DAY. MARIE PROULX."

Darren read it slowly out loud, again and again, until his voice was hoarse, long after the cell signal had disappeared. My bum knee had begun aching from the unaccustomed climb today, and I'd finally sat back down.

"Time for a beer," I announced and got two from the stash under the sink. "After all, if we're not the last two people on Earth, this might not be the only remaining six pack." I popped the caps off the Big Rock bottles and set them down on the kitchen table.

"Marie Proulx," Darren said, as if that was the most significant part of the message.

"The name rings a bell but I can't place it." I savored the bitter taste of the dark ale on my tongue.

"Yeah, you probably read about her in the news, the billionaire real estate woman who had her fingers in all sorts of Vancouver projects. A real venture capitalist. If anyone can save the world, she can."

"But a cell phone message?" I tried to think it through. "It's a big operation to run the things, isn't it? Generators, power plants, towers . . ." This was one subject where Darren might actually know more than me.

"There're these things called COWs, cell-on-wheels, like portable cell towers. I saw them at a concert once. Solar panels could be enough to power them. Maybe." He picked at the label on his bottle.

"But could the signal reach all the way from Vancouver?"

"Let's see. It's, what, about sixty kilometers, as the seagull flies? I seem to recall the range of the COWs was about thirty-five kilometers."

"And even if she got a tower up and running, why direct it this way? Vancouver and the rest of the lower mainland had millions of people. There's no one on these islands, never has been." Which is exactly why I'd chosen to retire here.

"Yeah, it doesn't make much sense but it's pretty awesome that she's done it." Darren put down his beer, still almost full. His eyes were shiny with emotion.

I drained my bottle and stood up. "Let's get some rest. Tomorrow, we're gonna work on those gutters. And we want to get the water barrels hooked up better before the late winter rains come. Carry us through the summer droughts."

"What?" Darren looked up at me, his voice shaky. "No, we need to build a glider or something. There's people out there. We need to—"

I cut him off. "You're forgetting something, Darren. I *chose* to be here. I *bought* this place with the intention of becoming self-sufficient. Off-grid. Technology's a trap. The world was a house of cards waiting to fall."

"Don't BS me, Mike." Darren was breathing heavily. He picked up the bottle opener and pointed it at me. "You're not self-sufficient when you need seeds, axes, water filters, a hundred things. You're not self-sufficient when the crops rot in the fields due to all this rain. Tell me, what you going to do when your shoes wear out?"

I kept my mouth closed. I had lists. Lists of seeds, tools, clothing, redundancy upon redundancy. If I'd stocked up, like I'd planned, it would have been enough. Enough for my lifetime anyway.

And I didn't care about anything beyond that.

Or anyone.

I put both hands on the table. "This doesn't change anything. My two boats are gone. Even if we had them, we don't have any fuel. We don't have a sailboat. If we did, we don't have any sailcloth. Since the quake, the tides are a meter higher than they used to be and the water in the strait is plain vicious." I pounded it home. "Anyhow, that text could just be a hoax."

"Bullshit! You just don't want to admit that there may be people out there. You'd rather they all died." Darren stabbed the bottle opener into the table so hard it gouged the surface.

I closed my bedroom door behind me and let the wind drown out his shouting. Stupid bugger. I should have told him to leave on his own, that the trip would be a piece of cake.

He wouldn't make it but, that way, I could have some peace and quiet.

‡‡

I heard the flapping before I entered the clearing. Like a hundred scoters taking off from the water or like a sailboat facing into the wind. I knew almost every inch of the island, from the new, higher shoreline to the marshy lake in the middle to the eagle's nest at the top of Lovat's Bluff. I was going as silently as I knew, down a well -used deer trail, rifle at the ready. Taking a buck would still leave a good sustainable population and fresh venison would be a treat. First, though, this fluttering noise. I stepped over a pile of fresh deer scat and edged around a huge Douglas fir.

An enormous rotting log, as high as my waist, dominated the clearing. A few stubby branches jutted up past leathery-leaved salal. On the far side, a white sheet billowed and snapped, high up near the crown of a cedar. I leaned my rifle against the log, the butt in a brown sludge of disintegrating maple leaves. Over the log and through some blackberries that tore at my jacket. The sheet was made of long narrow wedges of a thin synthetic material.

Like a parachute.

"Hello?" I called out, picturing a helmeted person impaled in the canopy far above me. Surely I would've heard a plane?

Only a varied thrush answered me.

I jumped up and grabbed the parachute, if that's what it was. Even if nothing was attached, I could always use another tarpaulin for the woodpile.

There was far more material than I could carry. And it wasn't a circle, like a parachute would be shaped, but more like a bag, a symmetrical bag.

It was a balloon. A large, rubbery balloon.

A corner of something metal poked out of the shrouds at the base of the cedar. I dropped the bundle of material and reached through a clump of late-season stinging nettles. The sealed metal box was about the size of a large suitcase but triangular and too heavy to carry far.

Darren needed to come see this. I was halfway back to the cabin before I realized I'd left the rifle behind.

"It's just over the next rise, almost to Lovat's Bluff. It's probably an old weather balloon or something," I said, shortcutting through a dense patch of salal. Darren jogged behind me, winded but managing to keep up. I used the crowbar like a machete, knocking honeysuckle vines and other irritants out of the way.

"Slow down, Mike, it's not going anywhere." Darren stopped, bending over and putting his hands on his knees.

I grunted. He was right. Why was I so fired up about this? In fact, if I thought about it, what I felt was *invaded*. You'd think, at the end of the world, the hordes would cease intruding.

"I want to get back before dark," I said. It was late afternoon and we had no lights with us—the last triple-A batteries for our headlamps had died a few days ago. And the woodstove would need refilling soon.

The casing on the triangular box came off with the first wrench of the crowbar. Inside were a battery and a tangle of wires and some other things I didn't recognize.

I moved aside so Darren could see. "What do you make of it?"

"Well, it's not a weather balloon, there're no instruments."

Oh. Right. I really was rattled or I'd have seen that.

"You know what? Mike?" Darren paused and looked at me. I stared back until he caved.

"I think it's a cell tower. Like, a portable one. Launched like a weather balloon. Hell, it may even be modified from one." He started talking faster. "Think about it. The balloon would go up thousands of feet. That would extend the cell reception range for miles, it would pass on a signal better than a tower. It'd be awesome!"

"Until the battery ran out." I kicked the metal box. The battery was a tiny little thing.

"Yeah. This must be a few days old. Marie must be launching one each day. Hey! That's why she said to respond at dusk! That's when there might be a signal!" He jerked his head up to look at the cloud-blurred sun. It was just touching the tips of the tallest firs. "We gotta head for Lovat's Bluff! That'll be the best reception! Quick!"

I didn't want another jog through the brush, especially toward a cliff top in the dark. I didn't want to go without dinner. And I didn't want to get home to a cold house.

I looked at his retreating figure, kicked the box one more time, and turned the other way toward home.

The rain started right after I'd gotten back to the cabin. When Darren came in, I realized I'd been staring at the black rectangle of the living window for quite a while. He stripped off his wet clothes while I pretended to read a flower identification guide.

The firelight made his face seem more gaunt, older, but his eyes were bright. He sank into the far end of the sofa. My old sweatshirt hung off his thin shoulders and his hair was still plastered against his head.

He grinned at me.

"Mike, I texted back and forth with them! Like, five or six times! Here, read all the texts!" He thrust the phone at me.

"Just give me the Reader's Digest version," I said, tossing down my book, settling back and putting my feet up on the coffee table. Whatever he'd found out, it wouldn't change anything.

"Marie's alive! She's got a team of about ten people, all techy types. The balloon thing we found is a portable cell tower with a range of about a hundred klicks. She was trying to send them inland where more people might be but the wind, you know, it's always from the southeast these days."

"And she just happened to have your number?" The fire had some handsome flames, putting on a show, all orangey and golden.

"She was sequentially dialling and texting that new area code that my phone uses, two-three-six? And she started with my exchange, you know, the first three numbers? The ones that fresh accounts are currently assigned to? That way, it would reach the newer handsets."

That almost made sense. It was how I might have done it. With automated equipment, it wouldn't take too long. Anyhow, it made a good story for a rainy night.

"She's asking every survivor she reaches to come to the university campus in Vancouver. She figures that if we all got through the flu this far, we're immune or it's mutated into a weaker form or something. One of her team is a professor, an epidemiologist." He stumbled over the last word. I got up and poured him a cup of herbal tea from the pot on the stove, adding a scant teaspoon of sugar from my stockpile.

"Thanks, Mike." He took a sip even though it was scalding. "She's trying all the ways she can think of to contact people, ham radio, landlines, even flares and fireworks. And these floating cell towers, as she calls them. Of course, even if people out there have cells, very few of them are keeping them charged." He looked up at me from under his eyebrows, waiting for a compliment.

"Huh." I got out my knife and a baggie of hawthorns. I began scarifying them, readying them for planting tomorrow. In ten years or so, I'd have a small grove of them. *Crataegus monogyna*: not strictly native but naturalized enough that I figured it wouldn't upset the wetland ecosystem down by the well. Alright for eating, plus a good source of ax handles.

"I told her we were coming." Darren put down his cup. "I told her we'd find a route. Build a sailboat. Find a way."

"Listen," I said, scraping a jagged cross on the blossom end of the small apple-like fruit. "Even if you got across the strait, there's the mountains on the coast. There'd be a long, long journey ahead."

He snorted. "You're not thinking outside your tiny little box. Why can't we fix the balloon and fill it with, I don't know, propane?"

"You kidding? Do you know anything about anything? The flammability . . ." I took a breath. I didn't even have to get technical to make him understand. "The balloon is only three meters in diameter. It can't lift more than a few kilos. And we only have the propane left in this lantern." I threw down my knife and picked up the lantern by its wire handle, nearly burning my fingers, and waved it, sending wild shadows arcing over the shelves and their jumble of books and papers.

The rolled-up topo map was just where I remembered it. I spread it on the coffee table, using hawthorns as weights in the corners.

"You'd land here." I jabbed my knife at the green-colored British Columbia shoreline right where the contour lines crowded together.

"Big deal! We get there and then we can hike to Vancouver," Darren said, too tired for his usual politeness.

"Okay, look at these elevations. Some of the ruggedest terrain in the world. Never had a highway because it's a jumble of mountains. About a hundred and fifty kilometers of steep, steep rainforest." My knife creased a line down the map, almost cutting through. "It's not gonna happen. We're better off staying here." I sat back, folding my knife.

"Here? So we can grow old and die?" He was practically sputtering.

"Drink your tea, Darren. What would you do in Vancouver anyway? For that matter, what would you be doing if the Wipe hadn't happened?" I pointed the knife handle at him. "Grow old and die, that's what. That's what life is *for*."

"Old man, you can rot here. I'm heading out in the morning." He lurched to his feet.

"Get us some firewood, there's a good lad."

He banged the cabin door so hard books fell off the shelves.

Darren was still there the next morning, huddled on the sofa, my old quilt wrapped around him. He had big circles under his eyes and his hair stood up in awkward tufts. A square red patch covered the knee of his now-dry suit pants, one of my old handkerchiefs. The stitches were precise and stitched as evenly as a machine would do it. It had probably taken him all night.

I put down the tool belt I was carrying. "Want to give me a hand with the gutters? A rush job before the rains come. You know the expression 'hurry up and wait'? That's how most chores are out here."

He crossed his arms and put his feet up on the coffee table with a thump. For once, he didn't say anything.

"Hey, take it easy," I said. "I don't like you much but I don't want you to throw your life away on something impossible. Maybe Marie Whoever can save the world. So let her. But don't start off on a fool's errand. You survived the superflu, the bombings, the quake, and the storms. Don't push your luck."

"Patience is a virtue, blah, blah, blah." Darren picked up the hammer and waved it. "Don't preach to me, old man. I taught retirement planning courses, remember? The stock market always rises. Eventually. Blah, blah, blah."

I took the hammer from him and picked up the tool belt. "There's probably something that I'm supposed to say right now," I said. "But I don't have any idea what it is."

Winter on the island used to be a joy. Lashing storms and howling winds are harmless and fun when you're in a cozy cabin with a good book. This year, when each piece of firewood had to be sawn by hand, when each bite of bread meant there was less flour in the bin, it was like the cabin itself was cringing when the rain beat at the windows and flooded over the roof like an endless, spiteful river.

Late January, it was cold enough to see my breath by dusk, cold enough for the rain to hurt when it hit. The drops thundered against my hood when I went out to fetch firewood before it was completely dark.

I stood in the driveway for a while, watching streams of water flow over the sparse gravel, forming deltas and islands, shaping the silt into patterns that blended and changed every minute. I'd got what I wanted, hadn't I? The world was leaving me alone. So what was my problem? Darren finally stuck his head out of the door and waved the lantern at me through the sheets of rain, like some kind of skinny worried lighthouse keeper.

Spring came, right on schedule. I was a bit surprised, in spite of myself, to see crocuses perk up the scraggly grass in the front yard and vanilla leaf lay its carpet along the creek bank. Winter had been a trial. We'd lost a few treetops on the Bluff, the crowns battered right off in the violence of the wind. A heart-stopping *whump* had woken us one night when an old growth fir had blown down, kissed the cabin roof, and smashed the kitchen porch. Darren took over the gardening, such as it was, and the baking, too. He was a surprisingly good cook. And I'd taught him to whittle. Once, I caught him leafing through my battered copy of *Walden Pond*. He rarely bothered to charge up the cell phone any more. The maps gathered dust on the shelf and our talk was mainly food and weather.

One particularly warm March day, I went down the shore trail to what was left of the dock. The thick planking had taken a beating in January and listed badly to one side. We'd spent a long day dismantling the kitchen porch, salvaging most of the wood, straightening the bent nails and I wanted to soak up the very welcome sunshine. I sat against a post, resting my sore knees, and admired the rocky shoreline and brilliant blue ocean. I'd bet it hadn't changed much in a thousand years.

"Cup of tea?"

I opened my eyes. I must have dozed off. Darren handed me the Perrier bottle full of cold yerba tea and sat, dangling his legs over the edge. He never liked it down here. I guess it reminded him of his plane crash. The storm had knocked the little Cessna into the sea like it was swatting a bug. His pilot had been killed instantly, the plane sunk a half a klick offshore and Darren had floated around for a while, clinging to his metal briefcase as it bobbed on the waves. He'd kind of come in with the tide, clutching the case against his chest.

"Thanks." I took a long slug of tea and watched an otter bobbing just off shore. It was unusual to see one by itself. Now *there* was an animal perfectly adapted to its environment. A little sun, a little fish, and it had a happy life.

"Think we salvaged enough boards for a root cellar?" Darren squinted at me and brushed his hair out of his eyes. He'd taken to tying it back into a stubby ponytail. I studied him for a minute. His sharp cheekbones caught the sun and his forearms below his raggedy rolled-up shirtsleeves were hard, the tendons taut above his scratched and dirty hands. No one would recognize him as an insurance agent now.

"You were right." I said, using the little speech I'd been rehearsing for a week or two. "We need to leave. Me choosing to be here is one thing. Stagnating here against our will is another."

"Leave? Where? To Vancouver?" Darren shifted on the rough boards. "But there hasn't been another text message. No more balloons. Nothing." He swung his feet back and forth. "You know they're probably all dead."

"We don't know that. We need to check it out." I swallowed the last of the tea and replaced the cap on the bottle.

"No. We don't." Darren shrugged. "I've adjusted. We can make it here. We *are* making it here." After a minute: "Why the change of heart?"

"I think I've adjusted too. I spent years wanting to be self-sufficient, wanting to blow off humanity." I paused. "I was wrong. I need people, whether I like it or not."

"So, I want to stay and you want to go. Kind of ironic." He elbowed me and laughed.

"You know what my tipping point was?" I let out a grin. "I used the last of the toilet paper this morning."

"Funny guy. Anyway, even if you got me to agree, how would we get there? Can't swim, can't sail, can't fly. There ain't no way." He put his hands flat behind him and leaned back so his face caught the sun. The otter dived, surfaced, and dived again.

"The boards from the porch, the old nails, some plans from a book I have, and a whole lot of swearing, that's how. Low tech wins the day. I build a little dinghy and some oars. It'll get us across the strait, then maybe we can baby it down the coastline for a bit. Might not have to hike through the mountains at all."

"Those dried up, splintery boards? They won't bend worth a damn. And waterproofed with what? Seagull spit?" His laugh was more of a bark.

"Son, it's for real. We're gonna do this."

"You, who never commits to anything?"

"Yeah, me." I grinned again. It felt good.

"It seems kind of all or nothing. You're sure a rowboat'll work?"

"Not sure at all. But I know we have to try. Build the boat and wait for a weather window."

"Hurry up and wait, eh." Darren twisted his mouth. This was the point in my speech where I thought he might be cartwheeling down the dock. Guess he *had* changed.

He kept silent so I added, "There're patterns that use flat boards. We've got two cans of contact cement to seal the hull with. If we layer on pieces of the balloon fabric I think it will work. We can do this, son." I tried to read his body language.

"Well, at least it won't be right away. I've got some cattail roots drying for flour. If I don't keep turning them over each day, they'll go moldy." He picked a splinter out of the dock and threw it in the water.

"Well, yeah, but it shouldn't take all that long. I've simplified one of the book's plans—"

He lifted a hand and gave me a lopsided smile. "Okay, sure, fine. You go ahead. I'll be here when you get back."

The otter swam away, heading back to its companions.

We both watched the ripples spread out behind the otter, travel to the dock, and lap up against the pilings beneath our feet.

I Shall Not Want

by KL Cooke

The day Sis got sick was like any around here. It wasn't even Easter yet, but hot enough that I woke up with the sun coming up and the flies at it already. They were buzzing around my face and bothering me and it was too hot to pull the sheet over my head to get away from them. Ma was in the kitchen downstairs, and it smelled good, like fried bacon always smells, but I knew there wasn't any for me. She only fixed it for Pa, before he set out for work. We got cornmeal mush and maybe an egg if there was any.

"Time you gotcher hide outta that bed," she said. "If'n ya wanna eat, git out there and look under them hens. An' take them buckets and bring me some water. An' tell Sis to git in here. She's been out in the kybo for goin' on half an hour."

The buckets were out on the porch, along with the yoke that always busted my shoulders. I just stood there a minute, because the air was so heavy it was hard to breathe.

"Git!" Ma hollered like she could see through the wall.

"I'm gittin,' Ma," I said, before she came out with the broom and started swinging it, like she was liable to do when she was mad about something, which was most of the time.

"Better be gittin! Gotta be good for somethin' 'roun here."

She was right about that. One leg in a brace and shorter than the other, I couldn't do much, even though I was old enough to be working like a man. I used to try, but Pa took it easy on me, and let me sleep in the mornings when he got up in the dark to do what he could before he had to head for town. Ma didn't think he should.

"He's gonna be a weakun all his life if'n ya treat 'im like a weakun."

Ma hated anything weak, and she got mad at people for being sick, like it was their own fault. She said she'd never been sick a day in her life, and I can't remember a time when she was. When she was in the family way with little Jenny, she kept working until the baby came out, and it seemed like she was hardly going to stop for that. Me and my brother Bill and Pa sat out in the barn all night in the cold, because there couldn't be any men in the house for a birthing. No men except for Doc Firestone, with Sis to help him, and a neighbor lady, Mrs. Carlisle. About three in the morning Ma started hollering like she was going to die, but then we heard the baby crying and Mrs. Carlisle came out and said we could go in now and see it, all shriveled up and looking like a squashed tomato. Ma was up the next day, down in the kitchen putting up jars, and Pa owed Doc five dollars.

That was about what he could make a week when he worked at Mr. McManus' brick yard, and Doc only took silver. He wouldn't take produce in trade because his people had to eat special food and he didn't have time to sell what people wanted to trade him. If he'd had a wife it might have been different, but she was dead. So Pa paid him off at half a dollar a week until the bill was settled, but he had to give him five and a half total, because Doc had to wait for his money and he had bills to pay too. Still, he was pretty good about letting people pay him when they could, because some docs won't come out at all unless you pay them up front in full. Ma said it was a crime and Pa shouldn't have called Doc Firestone in the first place, because all he did was stand around and put his hands out when the baby came and slapped its butt, and anybody could've done that. Some of the women around there brought in Beulah the Hoodoo Woman instead of Doc Firestone, because you could pay her in trade, and they said she was better than Doc at stopping the bleeding. Anybody who knew Ma, though, wouldn't figure she'd have truck with hoodoo, and as it was, poor little Jenny didn't last the winter.

Before I got the water I went to look for eggs and just took one of the buckets. The porch was starting to come apart at one end, something Pa had been meaning to get around to, but what with the corn and the tobacco and working for Mr. McManus at the brickyard, he never had time, and now that Bill was gone it was that much worse. That was another thing for Ma to get mad about. Everything was falling apart. The house must have been over a hundred years old. We didn't really know, because it stood empty for so long before Pa bought it. He bought it from Mr. McManus, and it took him ten years to save up enough, but it seemed like stuff came off faster than he could nail it back up.

On the way to the coop I thought I'd better visit the kybo for morning business, and that's where I met Sis coming back. Sis was older than me and Bill, and she was taller than me. I thought by the time I was fifteen I'd look down at her like Bill did, but that never happened, probably because of this damn leg. She looked drawn up and pale.

"I ain't feelin' good, Reese," she said. "I ain't feelin' good t'all."

"Don't be tellin' Ma that," I said. "She's madder'n a hornet this mornin.'"

"I know."

Inside the kybo there was still some of the stuff Bill used to write on the walls when he was sitting there. Stuff he thought was funny. Ma and Pa didn't think it was funny and used to make him wash it off, but he kept doing it anyway, because he was kind of a fool like that. Then after he died they left the last of it, I guess to remember him by.

> *There once was a farmer named Clyde*
> *Who went in the kybo and died*
> *His brother named Lou took and died in there too*
> *And now they IN TERD side by side*

Ours was only a one-holer, but that was pretty typical of Bill.

He got killed working at Mr. McManus' blasting powder and bullet works. They made the powder in some stone buildings down by the river where there was a mill race, and the one where they caked the powder had the roof blown off all the time. Usually nobody got hurt bad, but this time Bill was unloading at the magazine when it went. They heard it all over Paducah. Six workers including Bill were blown up to where all they ever found were pieces. Mr. McManus said it was probably their own fault, but he gave each family fifty dollars. Some of them said it should have been more, but the district judge said that was fair. Pa didn't say anything, because he wanted to keep working at the brickyard. He just took the money and I guess he was glad to get it, because old McManus didn't have to give him anything.

There were only a couple of eggs in the coop because the hens didn't lay much once the heat started and the creek ran dry. Me and Pa built that coop out of the parts of crates that Bill brought home from the powder works, and it was about the only thing on the property that wasn't falling down. The barn was as bad as the house. Pa tried to keep it up, but he was nailing good timber on rotten wood. It needed to be torn down and started fresh, but he didn't have the time or the money for that. Outside the planks were all silvery and splintered, and on one end there was a sign from a long time ago that said chew something tobacco, but you could hardly read it because most of the paint was gone. There was a hayloft were I hated to go up because you never knew if the floor was going to give way. There were three stalls, for Pa's saddle horse and the mules, and Pa kept the farm equipment inside, the plows and the hay rake. We didn't have a thresher, so we used to borrow one.

When Pa bought the place he thought he was buying the house and land, but he didn't understand the contract. It turned out he was only buying the house. We had the right to use the land, but we didn't own it, and we had to sell all the produce to Mr. McManus. Pa borrowed money from him too, so that he could plant and we had something to live on when the crops were coming in, and every year he got farther behind and deeper in the hole. He said that's why he didn't get me out of bed early to help him with the chores. He wanted me to have a rested head for school. He took Bill out of school when he was twelve so he could work, but he wanted me to pass the Eighth Grade Examination and go up to St. Louis and get a government job. Ma didn't like it. "Ya can't hoe with no book," she used to say, but this was one time Pa rode over her.

At that time I'd never been farther than Metropolis for the district fair, but Pa had been up to St. Louis on the river boat. There was a book in the school house that had pictures of St. Louis, and I couldn't believe there was anything like that, with all the people and big buildings, and the coaches in the streets that had engines that you ran by pushing a pedal. Pa said it wasn't like that anymore. It was like it is here, he said, only more of it, and all those big buildings were empty and the houses were gone. Most of the people were gone too, and the ones that were left had horses and mules, just like us, and I found out it was true. I knew we used to have coaches like that here, because you still saw parts of them around, like the one Jaime's folks used for a chicken coop, but I thought up in St. Louis they still had them.

They said there used to be a lot more people here in Paducah too, as many as twenty-five thousand, and I found that hard to believe, because there weren't more than five thousand in the whole district. Elder Willis said we were in the Tribulation before Jesus came back to set up the Kingdom of Heaven on Earth. In the meantime, Yahweh was punishing the people for following after the Whore of Babylon. I used to believe all that stuff that Elder Willis preached, but I don't anymore. I found out Pa didn't either. He said it didn't add up, because when he went down to the river he could see sea shells in the rocks. There's no sea around here, and they had to have been there a lot longer than Elder Willis said. Ma said Satan probably put them there to lead people astray, and Pa didn't argue with her about it, but later he said it all sounded like horse manure. That was when he was an old man in his fifties, and he said he wasn't scared to die because if there was a hell it probably wouldn't be any worse there than it is here.

When I got back with the eggs Ma was by herself in the kitchen.

"Sis feels real bad," I said.

"She done took to bed," Ma said. "Weakuns! Y'all a pack o' weakens!"

With Pa having to work at the brick yard, Ma would go out and hitch up the mules and plow herself. Now she didn't have Sis to help with the kitchen work.

I set out for school and met up with Jaime. That's how he spelled it, but he pronounced it Hi-may, like his pa's name that was spelled Jorge but pronounced Hor-hay. If some kid wanted to make him mad they'd call him Ja-mee, like he was a little kid or a girl, but if they did he was liable to fight, and he fought a lot. Probably that was because they were poorer than most people, even us. His pa was on the Posse when he got shot by some river rats. They used to come by in skiffs and tie up and loot what they could, and then take off again, all the way down to New Orleans to sell what they stole. Then they'd take a river boat back up and start over. They weren't like regular scavers who ran off if they saw somebody. The river rats did their thieving by force. This time the Posse caught up with them and brought them back. The district judge held a trial, and they hung them up down by the river. Mr. McManus made sure they stayed strung up there for a month, as a warning to any others who might come floating by and decide to stop. Elder Willis said that part was a disgrace, but most people agreed with old McManus, because just about everybody had lost something or someone to the river rats. After that Jaime's ma sewed clothes and took in washing to get by. He wanted to quit school and go to work for Mr. McManus, but she wouldn't let him. She wanted him to pass the Eighth Grade Examination, too, but it was going to be a long haul, because he wasn't too good at school.

Down the road there was a crab tree on the edge of a field.

"Look out," Jaime said, "'cuz I'll bet Roof's up in there."

Sure enough, when we got close the crabs started winging down at us. It was Rufus, but we called him Roof because he liked to climb up on everything. One time he climbed up on top of the school and knocked a bunch of shingles loose. Elder Willis caught him and took him back of the school house to give him a licking. When they came back Roof was smirking, but Elder Willis was crying. It always made him cry when he had to give somebody a licking, but he said he had to do it because Yahweh required it of him. Roof said it didn't even hurt.

He climbed down out of the tree with some of the crabs in his pocket and took a bite out of one of them.

"Whoa, dat sho is souh," he said after he spit it out.

"Wait'll they're ripe, fool," Jaime said.

"Time dey ripe Demmy John have 'em all."

Old Demmy John was a guy who used to go around stripping all the wild fruit he could find. He'd go in orchards too, if he thought he could get away with it. He made cider and brandy out of it, and probably could have made a decent living at it, except he drank most of what he made. You'd see him skulking around early in the morning or in the evening, but he never went into town because Mr. McManus had a standing order to lock him up on sight. The kids stayed clear of him, because if he could he'd grab you.

One time Ma caught him around our trees and he started cussing her until she hauled off and knocked him down.

The three of us were heading down the road, going slow because of me, until we got to the Haints. You didn't go slow there and I had to struggle to keep up. All you could see were some old buildings, but nobody knew what was in there, or if they did they didn't talk about it, but the first thing you learned when you were a kid was never go in. You could, because the fence around it was falling down, but nobody did. There were signs there from a long time ago with the skull and bones to warn you. Elder Willis said they did some kind of evil there that helped bring down the Tribulation.

Once we got past the Haints there was a field growing wild where we could see a woman out in the middle.

"Dat Beulah out dere," Roof said. "She gatherin' to make hoodoo. Dat lady gimme de creepers."

"Me too," Jaime said, but I knew his ma bought candles from Beulah. I saw one burning on a shelf when I was over at his house. They were jars full of wax with things painted on the side, and if you burned one all the way down it was supposed to bring you something you wanted or take something away. You didn't want to let Elder Willis find out you were doing that, because he said it was Apostasy and you might get disfellowshipped, but a lot of people did it anyway.

"My Pa's got a real powerful hoodoo," I said, "only he don't know how to work it."

"Oh yeah?" Jaime said. "What?"

"I'll show you sometime when nobody's home."

A while before that we were getting set to go fishing. Jaime had some hooks he bought off the men down at Mr. McManus' machine works. That was down by the river too, where he sold parts to the river boats and coal from his mine. The miners were prisoners the Posse rounded up, scavers and ne'er-do-wells and they'd come in on the wagons to unload the coal, wearing stripes and all chained together. The men at the machine works used to make fish hooks in their spare time and sell them ten for a dime, but it wasn't that often a kid had a dime to spend. When you did you'd go to the back door and holler in. Pa told me never to go in there because of all the belts coming down to turn the machines. One time a lady went in there to bring her husband his lunch and caught her hair in one of those belts and it ripped her head like a plucked chicken.

So we had the hooks, but we needed some line, and I thought there might be something we could use up in the attic and went to go look. It was tough climbing the ladder with this damn leg, but I made it up through the trap door. The only light up there came through a little window that had a shutter to keep the rain out. It was full of junk that might come in useful sometime, but the first thing I saw was Pa's big, rusty old trunk. I knew it was up there, but I didn't know what was in it because it had a padlock on it. Just for fun I pulled on the lock and the shackle came open, so I took it off, pried up the hasp and opened the trunk, even though I knew Pa wouldn't want me to.

Inside there was a bunch of old stuff that must've belonged to Pa's people before the Tribulation. There were pictures and papers and metal decorations attached to pieces of colored cloth. There was also this silver colored box, a little longer than a foot and not as wide, but real thin, like it wasn't built to hold much. There was a picture of an apple on it, all black with a bite out of it. I pulled on the lid, but instead of coming off it went back on hinges. The inside of the lid was glass, like a mirror, but it was black, and on the bottom of the box were rows of buttons, like dice, with numbers and letters. I pushed a few of them but nothing happened. I'd never seen anything like that before, but I knew it was a hoodoo, and that apple must mean the one Adam ate, and that's why we got the Tribulation and Satan ruling the world. I got spooked and put it back and closed the trunk. Later I told Pa what I did and asked him what it was.

"Reese," he said, "you know better'n to mess with things that ain't yer biz."

I did know better, because one time when I was little I got out his shotgun and was looking at it and he found out and gave me a licking. And he didn't cry about it either, the way Elder Willis did. I didn't get a licking this time, but what he told me was pretty strange.

"It's something from a long time ago, son, something from before your great grandpa's grandpa. It was in my pappy's stuff when he died and I kept it. It's a hoodoo, but ain't nobody who knows how to work it no more."

"Is it a haint?"

"I dunno. All my pappy tol' me is it's mighty powerful if somebody knowed how to git the hoodoo in it to work. Yer ma thinks it's a haint, and she don't want it 'roun here, cuz she sez it's an Apostasy. She sez if Elder Willis knew about it we'd get disfellowshipped an' yackety-yack, you know yer ma. Maybe she's right, but I ain't throwin' it out, because someday I'm gonna meet the man who knows how to work the hoodoo in it. He's gonna give me a nice bit o' silver for it, and we sure need that. In the meantime, dontcha lemme catcha messin' with it again, y' hear?"

"I hear, Pa."

When we got to the school house, which was next to the Meeting House, the kids were still playing out front, until Elder Willis came from around back to ring the bell for everyone to go inside. He stopped to wash his hands at the pump, because they were all covered with the white gypsum he used to make chalk sticks. He could've bought them off the riverboat, but he saved a penny wherever he could to keep the school running. Us boys gathered up rocks down by the river and helped him to crush it. He knew how to make black ink, too, but there was no way around buying the paper and pens, and he kept those under lock and key to keep them from walking away. The men of the Meeting built the school along with the Meeting House after the old one burned down. The old place was built out of scav a long time ago, but the new one was all fresh logs cut dovetail, so it didn't look like a pig pen the way most things around there did. They built the long tables and benches, too, with lumber that Mr. McManus had his men cut to size. He had them cut the slate for the blackboard too, and didn't even charge for it. Old McManus wasn't in the Meeting, or in the Holiness or any of the others, but he helped out with the schools. That way the folks who came to work for him knew how to read and pencil enough to get the job done, but not enough to figure out his lawyer writing.

The school only had one room, and all the kids sat together, from the little ones who were first learning their ABCs up to the ones like me and Jaime and Roof. I was the only one close to being ready for the Examination, so I was the only one writing with ink and paper. Before that I wrote on slate like the rest of them, but now that I was writing on paper I gave my slate to Jaime because it was better than the one he had that only had two sides. When I started school Pa made me one that opened like a book on hinges and had four sides. That way there was plenty of writing room for copy practice, and you didn't have to try and write small with the chalk, which is hard to do and still keep it looking neat. The men at the shop cut those slates for gratis too, and Pa fitted them with wood frames.

After we all took our seats there was the Morning Prayer, and after that the first thing was copy practice. That was the only thing we all did together, no matter how old you were. When Elder Willis was preaching he usually preached out of the Greek Scriptures, especially Revelation, but copy practice usually came out of the Hebrew Scriptures. The kids got their slates ready, and Elder Willis gave me a sheet of paper and an ink bottle and a pen. The steel nibs came all the way from St. Louis and cost a dime each, but you had to know how to use one if you were ever going to get a government job. He started writing the lesson on the blackboard for us to copy, muttering to himself when his chalk stick broke because he always pressed it too hard. We used to think that was funny and made faces at each other when his back was turned. We always hoped he'd slip up one day and cuss out loud, but he never did. He rolled out old Twenty-Three in a hand as nice as anyone could do with a chalk stick on slate that had pits in it.

> *Yahweh is my Shepherd, I shall not want.*
> *He makes me lie down in green pastures.*
> *He leads me beside still waters.*

And so on, all the way through the part about Goodness and Mercy who were supposed to follow me around all my life, like they were sheepdogs.

When I came home from school in the afternoon Sis was upstairs in her room in bed, and Ma wasn't fretting anymore about her playing sick to get out of work. I could tell she was worried now. I wanted to go up and look in on her, but Ma wouldn't let me.

"I don't need you comin' down with it too," she said, but still she went in and out like it couldn't get to her. It seemed like no sickness ever got to Ma, but me and Pa were on our own for supper that evening, and he made Indian pudding, because that's all we had that he knew how to make. The next day Sis was worse and it went on for a couple of days, until one morning instead of going to school I rode to town in the saddle behind Pa on his way to the brick yard. I was supposed to fetch Doc Firestone and ride back with him in his buggy.

Doc was away looking after somebody whose leg he might have to cut off, so I hung around town all day waiting for him. Folks asked me what I was doing and why wasn't I in school, because everybody knew I was getting ready to take the Examination, but I just made up stories because I didn't want them to know we had sickness in the house. When that gets around they start shunning you. Doc didn't get back until late, and he said he was dog tired and hadn't eaten all day, but after he had a chance to sit down for a while, and his housekeeper fixed him something to eat, he was ready to go again. By the time we made it back it was near sundown. Ma went up with him to look at Sis, while I waited in the kitchen. They were upstairs a long time. I heard Pa ride up, and after he put the horse away he came in and sat down at the table.

"What's Doc say?"

"Nothin' yet."

After a while they came back down and Ma poured some water from the kettle into a basin for Doc to wash his hands with soap he carried in his bag. Then he sat down with us at the table.

"Joe, Harriet you need to be strong for what I'm gong to tell you. You too, Reese. I'm afraid Clarissa has diphtheria."

"Oh Lord Yahweh," Ma said. Pa didn't say anything. Neither did I, but we all knew what it meant. Years before that there was an outbreak in Paducah and around the district. Hundreds of people came down with it, and about half of them died. It was before I was born, but we all heard the stories and saw how folks looked like they'd seen a haint if somebody even mentioned the word. Now it was like the Angel of Death had come to our door, and there was no blood mark to tell him to pass us by.

"I'm not definite, but I'm afraid so. I'll know for sure soon, but I'm quarantining the house. I need you to put a piece of black cloth on the door so folks'll know not to come in. And nobody is to leave the property. You can go to your fields, but that's it."

"But I gotta go to work," Pa said. "We're near busted, Doc."

"I'm sorry Joe, but you know the rules. I've got to let the town know, anyway, and then Mr. McManus won't let you anywhere near his place."

Doc Firestone said he'd come back the next day, but in the morning Sis was much worse. Her throat swelled up like a bullfrog and she could hardly breathe. It seemed like she was only half awake and her skin was getting a blue color. I wanted to go into town to get him, but Pa wouldn't let me.

"Folks know all about it now," he said. "Somebody sees you out running around they're liable to take a shot at you, boy."

Doc came by that afternoon. After looking at Sis he said her throat was closing over and he'd have to put a tube down her. Me and Ma held her down while he did it, but she was so weak she hardly struggled. Still, Doc had a tough time. He had something that looked like a little sickle with different blades that attached, and he tried them all before he got it to work and got a piece of rubber tube down. After that Sis quit gasping and the blue color started going away. But Doc said that wasn't the worst of it. He said her heart was starting to give out.

"Is she a goner, Doc?" Ma said. It was the only time I ever heard her sound scared.

"She needs horse serum, Harriet, and we don't have any."

"Horse syrup?" Pa said. "What in the world is that?"

"Serum, Joe, not syrup. It's a medicine made from horse blood. I know how to make it. I could use your saddle horse, but I don't have the right equipment. The only way to get it is to send up to St. Louis for it. If the Radio Office can get a message through to the college, they can send it down on a boat."

"Then do it!" Ma said. "Whatcha been waitin' fer?"

"What's it gonna cost," Pa said.

"That's just it, Joe. It's going to cost you everything you have, and even then it might not work. I'd say it's a fifty-fifty chance. To make it and send it down will cost five hundred dollars, and up at the college they won't do anything without getting the silver in advance."

Pa had been up pacing around the kitchen, but when he heard that he sat down, almost like his legs buckled under him.

"Five hundred?! I ain't got that kinda silver! This whole place ain't worth but about that, and even if'n I had it, how'd I git it to 'em? Time the next boat gits here Sissy's liable to be . . ."

He couldn't bring himself to say *dead*.

"I spoke to Mr. McManus for you, Joe. He'll buy back your contract for that much. He'll radio a draft to the bank in St. Louis."

"Then we'll be paupers," Pa said.

"Mr. McManus will let you stay on as tenants until he gets a new buyer. After that you can move into town."

"Tenants," Pa said. "I done worked my whole life for this."

"It's the best we can do, Joe."

"An' ya say she's liable not to make it anyway?" Ma said.

"Fifty-fifty, Harriet."

After Doc Firestone left we went to bed. There wasn't any sense in wasting candles with nothing to do. After a couple of hours I woke up when I heard a noise coming from up above me in the attic. I used to hear noises from up there all the time, because squirrels got in there, and raccoons, but this wasn't the sound of varmints rustling around. There was somebody up there moving things. I got out of bed in the dark, opened the door and looked down toward the end of the hall where the ladder was. The trap door was open and I could see the flickering light of a candle, so I climbed up the ladder, pulling myself up by my arms because of this damn leg. I had to find out what was going on. It was Ma up there. She'd opened Pa's trunk and taken out the silver box and had it sitting on the trunk lid with a candle in front of it. It was one of Beulah's candles with painting on the jar. Ma heard me and turned around.

"Better not say nothin' 'bout this boy, y' hear!"

In spite of Elder Willis she was doing Apostasy, trying to get Sis well with Pa's hoodoo. It didn't work, though, and she died, even before he could make up his mind about what to do.

SHIFTING GEARS
BY CATHERINE MCGUIRE

MERRIDEL WOKE TO THE SOUND OF CHICKADEES chorusing beyond the shutter. It was another gorgeous spring morning, but Merridel, in her autumn, couldn't find the usual swell of enthusiasm. Recently, the days seemed to drift by, each one the same. Then she remembered—Jarvis should be coming through today! She had to get the library order ready.

Quickly but quietly, she put on her knee-length green tunic and knitted stockings, leaving Julia asleep in their featherbed. Some days she envied her partner's job; being mayor didn't start till well after dawn. Honestly, neither did librarian, but an early start meant she didn't fall as far behind.

Merridel paused at the alcove shrine to give thanks for another day and ask Gaia's assistance finding the right path. In the kitchen, she made do with oat bread and hard cheese—it was too much trouble to pump water. But she packed slices of dried meat and a small bag of dried mint. She could heat tea water later in the solar cooker she used to make book glue, if the sun cooperated. She washed her face and combed her unruly salt-and-pepper curls, examining her face in the polished tin mirror, for once glad the metal was too dim to show details like wrinkles.

They lived in a cob duplex two blocks from the library and shared a vertical garden with neighbors. This time of year, the canted shelves for plantings were still empty except for some wintered-over garlic and kale, but espaliered cherries and plums were flowering along the fence, and their perfume finally pushed Merridel's mood up. She loved spring, but this year she feared she couldn't muster the energy for its many obligations. Group plowing was so much fun, as was the scion swap—a chance to meet with townsfolk and other towns. But all the little tasks—weeding, watching for bugs, protecting from frost—took more and more energy. She tried to shake off her negativity and picked up her pace.

At the end of the gravel lane, the merchant shops began: candlemaker, weaver, wool store, and the Mercantile taking up half of the far side of the street. Merridel noticed Lars unloading his bright green single-wheeled goat cart; the brass milk cans fit compactly on both sides of the large wooden wheel. And Sahra was walking up with three racks of eggs balanced on her head for Abas, who was happy to allow consignment where he didn't buy outright. That reminded her to bring down her latest batch of scrap paper notebooks and quills—there was a surprising market for them. She waved to Sahra and held her breath as the girl waved back while keeping the eggs steady—she'd never be able to manage that.

It was just after dawn, but she could hear shutters thumping open, the humming of people at their prayers, the squeaky wheels of the compost cart as it did the morning pickups. Other early blooms spread their perfume, mixed with dust and the sharp cut-cedar tang from the carpenter's workshop on the next block. Merridel loved this time of morning, before Salvage Grove got too busy, noisy and dusty, when she could believe she had a chance of getting through her whole day without falling behind.

When she reached the library, she pulled the large iron key from her pocket and fought with the old lock. She'd asked the Council twice already to fix the complicated mechanism. One of these days she'd have to saw through a window shutter to get in! One of the first shingled cobs put up fifty years ago when the town was founded near a prime resource site, it had survived well, but like Merridel herself, it was somewhat worn. She crossed the main room by feel, avoiding low shelves of books, a pair of round tables with their straight chairs, and the small cart with wheels that allowed her to re-shelve books without wearing out her sandals. She reached the desk, and leaned in to turn the shutter pole—as she cranked the brass rod, the roof shutter mechanisms slid open and dawn outlined the room.

It was only ten feet by twenty feet, a small collection of books and some old sheets of paper too fragile to handle. There had been so little salvaged from the first chaos, when the unimaginably long supply chains and power lines broke and every area was cast out on its own. The cities' tall steel and concrete towers had become death traps—salvagers still found bones in the rooms. Those who fled from the cities started from scratch. The few ancient survivors refused to talk about it, and everyone had agreed to put it behind them. There were no books in here that detailed the destruction—those who'd tried to save history were far more concerned with finding paper versions of the vast information that had been on their magic machines. There were a few books of warnings, but half of the items didn't make sense. Don't let GMO corn mix with heirloom? Avoid low EMF frequencies??

Merridel tried to focus on the task at hand. Jarvis came by monthly with his wooden printing press compactly stowed in his hide-covered cart. He would stay the day to print up marriage certificates, birth certificates and the like, but for books like Merridel's, he'd take the aging copy and have it reprinted next time. She was looking forward to seeing *Growing Winter Vegetables* again, and she had to be sure she had all the pages of the herbal text that had finally fallen apart from overuse. About half the books here were handwritten—she employed three scribes—but some books were popular enough that getting five copies per order was worth the cost. If paper and ink were more available, there'd be no limit to how many books Jarvis could print! She suspected he printed extras to sell to other libraries, since he always brought a few new books to entice her with. But not only did she have a limited budget, this town was strict about info. One of the deadliest problems of the Oil Culture was too much information—it had confused, agitated, and ultimately destroyed them. Now, only recognized facts were allowed to be circulated, and only sustainable processes shared. There were no unlimited resources; paper and ink were allocated only to the most useful words.

A clattering, huffing noise from the street sent her to the front door. As she leaned out, she saw most of the other shopkeepers doing the same. At the end of the road, a cart was jerking forward slowly . . . without horses or mules. Squinting, she recognized it as Jarvis', and wondered whether he had somehow put his cart before the horses. But there was steam coming from the back, swirling up into the sky. Just as the thought *machine* entered her mind, she saw Raul on his bicycle heading down the street to meet the printer.

"Oh, turd," she muttered, closing the door behind her and hurrying up the street. She met up with them just as Raul was ordering Jarvis to shut off the motor.

"You are hereby ordered to cease and desist the use of a prohibited device," Raul began. Merridel stepped closer and put a hand on the diminutive hawk-faced teen's shoulder. Thankfully, he shut up.

"Jarvis—I'm very glad to see you," she said hurriedly, "but I'm surprised not to see Bucky and Ebony."

"We had a bad patch over at Glory," Jarvis said, leaning down from the bench. He was only a little younger than Merridel, sunburnt to mahogany with wrinkles that could almost be woodgrain. His hair was snowy and he wore his ink-stained uniform: a white cotton cap, blue denim overalls, and a pale green linen shirt. "Nearly the whole town's nags died of something, and mine too, since I was there. But some clever gent got me hooked up with a wood-gas engine and away I went." He grinned; the gaps in his teeth made her wonder, as usual, how he managed to chew his food.

"Wood-gas engines are machines, and thus are prohibited within town boundaries," Raul insisted. "He needs to be gone within the hour."

"And he will be, Raul. Especially if you just let us get our business done." Merridel regretted her sharp tone, because the boy was just doing his job. But she needed this printing! "He's going to park in front of the library and he'll be gone within the hour. Thank you, Raul."

She gestured to Jarvis to keep going and she waved at all the busybodies who were still gawking from their doors. And she resisted putting her fingers in her ears as she returned to the library, even though the sound was really obnoxious. She'd never heard anything so ratchety before. The grist mill's waterwheel was loud but soothing, the rasp of hand saws could be annoying, but this was like the Death of Metal. As the cart passed, she saw the metal device: two upright cylinders connected with pipes and a small box—steam was coming from the top of the pipes. If *this* was what machines were like, no wonder they had been prohibited! Raul was speeding off in the direction of the City Council building, so she knew who'd be coming back soon.

She'd have to do business with Jarvis in the street or neighborhood children would be all over the cart. She waited until the old man had gotten off his bench before she started. "Jarvis, I'm surprised you didn't remember this is a sustainable town," she said, having to shout. "And it *does* say on the signs at the edge of town."

"Well that just shows y'all don't understand—if this horse plague comes through, y'all will be left without transport," he retorted. "Unless y'all can push your own carts."

"Let that go for now. Do you have my printing?"

He reached behind his bench and pulled out a wooden box, opened it on the bench and handed over one sheet after the other—Merridel was thrilled to see the sharp, uniform letters cleanly printed on each page. And there were fools in town who wanted to call Jarvis' press a machine! Luckily, since it was hand-powered— basically a wine press with a tray of metal letters beneath—it passed as a tool. As she checked to be sure no pages were missing—a bit tricky, since they were laid out for folding into signatures—she was disappointed to see that some of the paper was lumpy, not the usual good quality. It might be harder to bind and get them to lie flat. But Jarvis didn't make the paper, and it wasn't bad enough to reject them.

"They're well printed, as usual," she acknowledged. "I'll go get payment, and I have another book for you. Wait here." As she hurried inside, she wondered if she would lose this herbal—how could she get it if he couldn't come back? *I suppose I could meet him at the edge of town*, she thought, rummaging around in the cashbox for five brass dollars, then picking up the wrapped herbal.

Outside, Marshal of Peace had arrived with two guards. Thoma was a tall, thin man with thick black hair that brushed his shoulders, a wide, crooked nose, mud-brown eyes under bushy eyebrows and long gnarled fingers that were constantly active, brushing or picking lint. He was acting as if this was some kind of contagion! It wasn't like someone could copy an engine like this with one glance.

"Good morning, Thoma," she said, forcing cheerfulness. "Jarvis was just leaving."

"It's a good thing," the Marshal replied, his scarecrow body radiating scorn, his caterpillar eyebrows arched. "We'll just escort him out of town."

Merridel fumed, but there wasn't much she could say. Instead, she turned to the old man, thanked him profusely and said, "Next month, let's meet down at the Inn outside of town."

"But what about my certificates?? There's lots of people waiting for me . . ." He glared around Thoma and the two burly guards for a moment, then sagged. "Y'all be sorry," he said, and got back onto his cart.

Merridel didn't watch him roar down the street with the guards trotting to keep up—she went back inside and stared at the new printed sheets without seeing them. She certainly wouldn't argue that a machine *that* noisy had no place in town— imagine a half-dozen of them roaring and sputtering down the streets! But it wasn't just Jarvis—lately, several itinerant merchants had been caught with "contraband" and disinvited from town. Salvage Grove had started out scrambling like every other town, but in the last twenty-five years had settled into a manual and passive system mandate. And as others rediscovered bits and pieces of the Oil Culture, Salvage Grove was fielding one conflict after another.

The door opened suddenly. She spun around, but it was only her copyists—Dora, Lilluan and Yallow, almost interchangeable teens with the stylish multi-braid hairstyle and long tunics of blue and white checks. Only their elaborate embroidered belts distinguished them. They were chattering excitedly and Dora called out, "They caught a machine inside town! It was noisier than a metal bed frame falling down stairs!"

"I know," Merridel said. "That was our printer—so no more books or certificates until we find someone who uses a horse and cart."

"Oh no!" Lilluan wailed. "I was getting my choice certificate printed!!"

"Well, you could probably catch him if you run," Merridel said dryly. "They can't stop you outside of town. Though he's probably angry enough not to do business."

"Don't worry, Lilluan," Dora said, patting her arm. "Rita does a gorgeous certificate and she even paints tasteful little pictures of the tits and groin."

"I know, but I can't afford her! It would be at least six dozen eggs or a whole brass dollar! Jarvis prints them for a couple pennies."

"Yeah—he has the whole thing set up except for the name and sex, and he hammered those lead pieces in and printed it out faster than I could pull out my coins," Yallow agreed.

Merridel shooed them over to their desks, and adjusted the mirrors to maximize the incoming light. "If you three practiced your handwriting, maybe *you'd* get business doing calligraphy certificates. Today I will be happy with legible copies."

She heard Dora sniff in disdain but she ignored it. The foolish chits were so distracted with dances, weddings and preparations for the spring festival that she'd be lucky to get any work out of them today.

She went back into the tiny one-window closet she called her office, opened the shutter and adjusted her own mirror, trying to focus on her request for town funding, but Jarvis and his crazy machine invaded her thoughts. She could understand Council not wanting townsfolk using the dangerous machines from the Broken Time, but surely they were cutting their own nose off to insist anyone, even their trading partners, be "pure handcraft." And what happened to "the varied ecosystem of ideas"?

She looked up as the front door opened and the sound of laughing children filled the library. This would be Ronnie's fifth-grade class, in for the geography lesson. Maps were some of the things just too expensive to reproduce, so it was easier to come to the maps. She went to her doorway and waved at Ronnie as he ushered the children around the tables and retrieved the two large atlases from the oversize shelf. She enjoyed watching them ask questions about the world, even though these days answers were "scarce as silk." Still, landmasses didn't change, and if their society didn't die off from famine or plague, someday they might actually reconnect with the lands across those giant oceans. It was a mind-boggling thought.

Her apprentice Suberry had come in with the class and was processing the books that had been returned yesterday. A quiet, shy young woman, she was a perfect match for a library. She nodded at Merridel and kept on with her work.

Merridel shook herself out of her woolgathering and gathered up the manuscript pages. The bindery was an adjoining room, not much bigger than her closet office, but with a slanted, glass-paneled roof to maximize the light, and chest -high tables to minimize bending. She'd had the woodturner make a small bookpress and a stitching frame, and she mixed her own glue, using mucilage from the Rosedale renderers. It was finicky work, but she enjoyed it, and enjoyed the result even more. She wished she could afford leather, but Shereen's fine-woven linen was durable enough. Over thin wood boards, it made a beautiful book cover, especially with the title batiked on.

Again and again Jarvis's noisy cart and Thomas' scorn played in her head. She started making mistakes—cutting the waxed thread too short, folding a page slightly crooked. And the sun kept ducking behind clouds, making an uneven light.

I can't afford to mess this up, she thought, and set it aside. Impulsively, she decided to send a message to the librarian of Rosedale—Jarvis would head there next. As far as she knew, Rosedale wasn't nearly as strict, but it was worth warning Laurel.

By now the streets were full of life—the shop fronts were opened and tradesmun were working on their crafts while keeping an eye open for shoppers. Shereen had brought an upright loom to the front beside the open double doors, while behind her Denio tinkered with her four-harness shuttle loom. He seemed to be replacing some of the reeds, and as Merridel wandered over for a closer look, he straightened up with a guilty look on his face.

"Morning, Merridel," he said. Was he shifting to hide something?

"Were you finally able to repair the loom?" she asked. Now Shereen had turned and was looking at her also. Was she imagining some slight defensiveness?

"It took a while, but yes," Denio answered, brushing himself off as he came out to the sidewalk. "Now Shereen will be able to get some good yardage done."

"Aye," she chipped in, "once it's warped, I do a couple yards a day, and I've got five people waiting for summer linen."

"Well, you do fine cloth," Merridel answered. She bent over to examine the blue and white striped linsey woolsey half-finished on the frame. Out of the corner of her eye, she saw a brown paper wrapping by the other loom—the printed label read "Bamboo Reed Manufacturers, New Chitown." So Denio had purchased those reeds; probably machine-made. That's what he was hiding. Not that she cared. She nodded brightly. "I'm sorry to have disturbed you. Use the light while it's strong. Good day."

Merridel picked up her pace and then ducked into the telegraph office. Marcia the operator grinned up at her without losing the flow of the message she was tapping out. Merridel waited, looking around the tiny office, which flickered as sun danced through clouds overhead, sending shafts in and out of the light well. Behind the half-wall between the desk and the front area, there was only the operator's desk, a hand-drawn map of the telegraph route linking a dozen towns, and a filing cabinet. On the half-wall were scattered small framed wax boards to write out the messages. And to think they used to throw away whole garbage pails full of paper with only one side printed, sometimes only read once! She picked up a thin stylus to compose her message. Maybe she should ask Laurel to report what Jarvis said about the encounter—she might have to bring a small gift to him next month. At a penny a word, would it be easier just to set up a meeting with Laurel at the seedling market next week? Yes, and that would be a good excuse to go. She wrote up her request, finishing just as Marcia ended the transmission. The young blonde lurched to her feet, rounded with a pregnancy that should be ending soon.

"Morning, Merridel," she rasped. Some childhood throat illness had almost destroyed her voice, so few were surprised when she ended up learning the telegraph and also assisted the teacher with the deaf language classes. And she had married the deaf bakery assistant, one of many who were born impaired, the result of hidden poisons that were a "gift" of the Oil Culture.

"Good morning, Marcia," she said. "When is the happy day?"

"Should be near Equinox," the girl croaked. "That's eight pennies."

"Put it on the library account, if you don't mind."

She was in a thoughtful frame of mind as she headed home for lunch. Obviously she wasn't the only one having to contort themselves to work around town strictures. Maybe there was another Revision coming—the last one, twenty years ago, caused a third of the townsfolk to move away, after they couldn't agree on how many parts separated a tool from a machine. Granted, in the gray areas, it was sometimes difficult to tell. The doctor's foot-pumped bellows, used to help those with lung flu hang on until the body healed itself, had several very finicky parts and some had protested, but the blacksmith, whose father had been saved using the lung-pump, argued that it was no different than his own bellows, only smaller and more delicate. In the end, they'd agreed to allow it. Now perhaps there'd be an argument about whether to import machine-made parts, as long as the town tools were hand-constructed and repaired.

She was surprised to find Julia at home, removing a pot of hot soup from the rocket stove. Two bowls were set on the table, and plate of bakery rolls on the counter. Julia's coppery brown ringlets bounced forward on her high latte cheeks; long lashes hid her brown eyes as she pursed her lips in concentration.

"How is mayoring going today, love?" Merridel said, leaning for a peck on Julia's cheek. Her partner only came up to her shoulder, yet somehow towered in the relationship.

Julia put the pot on the table. "Funny you should ask that," she began. Merridel tensed. She couldn't have heard about Jarvis so soon?? But Thoma could never resist bragging about his little victories. "I heard you had an unusual visitor today."

"No—just the printer. It's true he came without his horses."

"And you prevented them from escorting him out?" Julia asked as she ladled out a tomato corn soup that Merridel had put up last fall.

"I did not! That little bicycle bully insisted Jarvis be out of town within an hour and our business barely took ten minutes. And then Thoma marched him out like he was a leper." Merridel fumed—she had wanted a quiet meal to help digest the morning. This was making it worse. She dipped a hunk of bread in the soup and nibbled it. "Look, if you don't mind, could we not fight over our meal? It's lovely to see you here."

"We weren't fighting. At least I wasn't. But fine—" Julia waved her hand and changed topics. "What should we get for Allen and Aruna's wedding?"

"I think Allen had his eye on the apple punnet over at the Merc. We might be able to afford that."

"I'm not worried about the tradecost—my brother only gets married once."

With luck, Merridel thought, since Allen was one of the Divine's great curmudgeons—never met a person he couldn't argue with. She hoped Aruna knew what she was getting herself into.

"Another thing," Merridel said. "Jarvis mentioned today that the horses of Glory died of some plague. It took out his two also. You should look into that—we don't need something exterminating our work horses."

"I'll get Marcia to telegraph—with luck it was just some bad feed or water. Though we might have to ban visitors from Glory for a while." Julia dropped her spoon and cursed—she was more tense than Merridel had seen her in a long time.

"How could we tell? Without medical tests, we're guessing."

"We can still make good guesses. For example, if the dead horses didn't consume the same things, or if the illness spread in a way that suggested contagion."

That was one of the things that made Julia good at her job. She was logical and good at detail. Merridel was just good with her hands, and often found herself arguing both sides of the question without coming to any conclusion. She almost told Julia about the imported reeds, then stopped herself. Julia didn't need any more trouble.

Merridel finally got down to work after noon, letting the rhythm of bookbinding settle her nerves, listening to the whispers and giggles of the fourth grade English class as Suberry read them an old story of an orphan boy named Huck. She had just put the first two signatures into the stitching press when the front door slammed open and a moment later, Nurmi, a messenger boy, paused in the doorway to catch his breath.

"Mayor says . . . Mayor says to come . . ." He was gasping. Merridel ran to him.

"Is she at the Council offices?" Divine Grace, not at the doctor's clinic!

Nurmi nodded without speaking, and after a quick glance to be sure nothing was left in a dangerous state, she raced around him, out the door and down the street.

She was winded before she arrived at the City Council office four blocks away. It was one-story, cob-built, filling an entire block. Merridel waved to the town clerk and hurried back to Julia's office, a room twenty feet on either side and well-furnished with deep window seats, a plain pine desk and four straight-back chairs set around an oval table. There were bookshelves with the bound records of Council meetings arranged chronologically. Nothing looked askew; no blood on the floor—Merridel took a deep breath and took in those assembled: Julia, Thoma, the engineer's apprentice Dale, his parents and two members of the Council, Venkat and Mare. She frowned and stepped inside.

"We ask that you be Witness, as a town member," Julia said quickly. Her partner's expression was a blend of real panic and phony officialism. Beside her, Thoma looked smug; the council members looked skeptical at her "convenient" appearance. Dale was looking down, his straight black hair obscuring his face. His parents, both about his shoulder height, seemed confused and angry.

So this was some kind of infractions hearing. Merridel's chest tightened—sixteen-year-old Dale was a brilliant lad, but forever tinkering where he shouldn't be.

Thoma announced, "Dale Affray, you have been charged with an illegal machines act contravention, which carries a penalty of five hundred dollars or three months field labor."

Merridel gasped, and Dale looked up, protesting, "It was just a few brass rods! I didn't make anything different. I just connected—"

"You created a machine to circumvent manual labor," Thoma interrupted, "by making the bike-powered thresher work on its own. Do you deny this?"

Dale's father groaned and Dale looked down again, and shrugged. "No. . . . But all I did was connect it to the grinding wheel by the river. If water can power the grain mill, why can't it power our thresher? We're all getting tired of that bicycle job."

"It's not for you to decide, Dale," Julia said. Merridel winced—Dale was a boy with a good heart, a sharp mind . . . and no sense. But this punishment was too much!

"If I may speak?" she tried, but Julia waved refusal.

"Witnesses can only witness, please you," she said formally. Merridel fumed—*why was I called here then?* She could've grabbed anyone off the street. She paused and considered that. There *must* have been a reason—Julia wanted her to see this. But what could she do??

She knew Julia couldn't step out of her role and take sides, nor could she impart secrets from Council meetings—but as a Witness, Merridel was free to draw conclusions and make citizen complaints. And it certainly seemed to warrant that. Was Thoma taking his frustrations out on the boy, after today's incident? Or worse —was Thoma starting to get a little crazed in his anti-machine stance? But if she was going to make a complaint, she needed to know more about the situation.

"As Witness, I am allowed to request more details of what I am witnessing," she said firmly, and was answered with Julia's smile. She must be on the right track.

Thoma looked thundery, but he recited from memory: "Defendant was discovered with a threshing machine powered not by human pedaling, but by a series of brass rods that extended from the pulley belt out along a field and down to the river, to the gristmill mechanism."

"I saw it in an old magazine about oil pumps," Dale interrupted. "All I did was attach rods that reproduced the motion at a distance. If the gristmill is an acceptable use of water power, then attaching it to the bike pulleys can be—"

"The defendant will be silent!" Thoma bellowed. Definitely taking his job too seriously. Maybe she needed to start a campaign to elect a new peace marshal.

"This Witness is minded that the penalty for abuse of office is removal," Merridel said sharply. "Thank you for the information, you may proceed." If he was going to act like Generalissimo Machismo, she could get formal, too.

He stared at her for a long moment, then turned to Dale. "As this was a first infraction, I have decided to fine you one hundred dollars or one month field labor."

Dale looked at his parents, blushing deeply, then looked at Thoma. "I don't have money, so I'll do the labor."

Merridel filed out with the others, torn between talking privately with Julia and not pressing her special status. There'd be time later.

"Where did he get such information, I wonder?" Mare said. She stopped, held the door for Venkat and teased, "Age before beauty, sir."

"And it would be impolite, I suppose, to suggest we are of an age?" he replied, grinning. "Merridel—could this information have gotten past your Guild?"

"I'll have to look into it—it sounded like he was stating there *was* no new technology—just connector rods. I definitely will investigate further," she assured them, then hurried back to the library.

The Editorial Guild had been feeling pressured recently, reading through newly -excavated material quickly in order to get it on the shelves. Merridel hated the idea of censorship, but if it was going to happen, she wanted to be on the committee. Perhaps they had overlooked something? But if Dale was accurate, he was implementing a variation, like the small bellows. What had gotten Thoma's back up? On impulse, she ducked into the Mercantile. If anyone knew, it would be Abas, the town gossip.

The store was one of the few timber buildings, crammed with old and new merchandise, both on the shelves and piled on the floor. Merridel paused to let her eyes adjust to the dimmer light created by pas-sol bottle lamps inserted into the ceiling. Abas had a few window mirrors, but piles of merchandise blocked the light. The left side of the huge room was salvage: bottles, chairs, wheels, hoes—all of the excavated metal, plastic, glass, and miscellaneous that was still usable. The right side was new, with sections for food, clothing, raw materials, furniture and tools. Abas held court in the middle, behind a square wooden counter that guarded valuable items that might tempt the foolish to fast-finger them. The shopkeeper was scolding his apprentice Marva, shaking a small wooden box of broken glass. She waited until he had sent the girl into the back room with the command not to break anything else before she approached.

"Good morning, Abas, may the light of the Divine shine on you," she said, bowing slightly.

"And on you. How may I help our librarian today?" Abas leaned forward; his five -foot frame made the counter chest-high, but he had the energy of a baby goat or a tightly-wound clock spring. Jovial, but Merridel would hate to work for him.

"I'm wondering if you've gotten the mucilage from Rosedale?"

"Alas, I think not, but I will look." He led her to a shelf containing powders, pastes and small brown glass bottles of the few chemicals allowed to be imported.

"Did you hear the noise when Jarvis arrived?" she asked.

"One would have to be deaf to miss that! Has the printer sold his horses for mucilage?" he joked.

"He said there was a horse sickness in Glory."

"The Divine spare us! What we need are those magic potions that cure sickness —have you found any of those in your old books?"

"Not yet, although we are always looking for new allowable solutions. Thoma got rather huffy about Jarvis today."

"Between you and me, Thoma is afraid of losing his position," the shopkeeper replied, tapping his long nose and winking. "I have heard the Council wants to create a Department of Innovation to investigate the new discoveries that have been cropping up recently."

"And Thoma wouldn't be included?"

Abas shook his head. "He would focus on keeping the peace only."

"I'll bet that would feel like a step down," she commented. It would be enough for him to increase enforcement to impress the Council. Merridel assured Abas there was no rush on the glue powder, and returned to the library, needing to think.

She wasn't in favor of another committee—Divine knew, there were enough already! And Julia would likely be required to sign off on minutes, at least—more work. But maybe Thoma's increasing belligerence worried the Council also. Was there such a thing as doing one's job *too* well? Some nearby towns "ruled from the rear," allowing citizens to use anything and only forbidding what proved harmful. They seemed to be doing alright, but Merridel had read enough old manuscripts to know that approach had its dangers. Where was the balance?

She checked the shelves in the science section, familiar with most of the books and papers, but unfamiliar with Dale's project. Finally, in a thick, hand-scribed manual, an illustration of rods extending between odd devices caught her eye. She scanned the words and although not mechanical-minded, got enough to agree with Dale. This was a variation on pulleys, which were fully allowed. Thoma had overstepped when he accused without first checking the details. But how had Dale gotten this? Merridel didn't remember seeing him in the library. In any case, a complaint was warranted. And maybe that new committee *was* needed.

‡‡

That evening was an Outreach Guild potluck; Julia, as mayor, would attend. And Merridel, as partner, should at least make an appearance. She sighed—she wasn't much for politics. But outreach to other towns, to wandering tradesmun, would affect Jarvis and the other situations. Thoma was sure to be there. So after work, Merridel trudged back to the Council offices. The buffet was in the largest chamber, with its yellow-washed plaster walls and simple concave molding. The west-facing windows were radiant and the lightwell provided more illumination. Tables were pushed against the walls and chairs grouped in small circles, already full of Guild members and guests. Even though it was Spring scant-time, there was a savory variety of preserved foods along one table. Merridel's mouth watered at Vencat's pickled beans and Albas' spiced salt beef.

The Guild was hosting Fuller's Bend, an even more restrictive town—all Church of Christ Survivor—ten miles upriver. The Bend representatives were identically dressed in indigo tunics, wide pants, cropped hair and no body adornment. Merridel knew they frowned on transfolk, because several had moved here before coming out, but the lack of clothing and grooming differences—the men were clean-shaven—almost gave them a uni-sexual look. Except for the hefty gray-haired woman with enough bosom for three. They were solemn as they chatted with Guild members, not straying far from each other. "Circling the wagons," they used to call it.

Before she could fill a plate, Julia tapped her on the shoulder and gestured her into the adjoining scribe's room.

"Thoma is threatening to invoke another Revision!" Julia exclaimed, on the edge of tears. "I don't want the town pulled apart on my watch!" She sank into a chair, and put her face in her hands.

Merridel patted her shoulder uneasily. "Rumor has it that he's being eased off technology decisions. Is this about power?"

"Ha!" Julia burst out, then realized Merridel wasn't punning. "I can't tell if he's just self-important or really an ideologue. Either way, he's threatening to ruin my tenure."

Merridel was more worried about the town than her partner's status. She liked things the way they were. But that was the problem, wasn't it? Things never stayed the way they were.

"It's true that traders are using or selling some new devices—the horseless cart, the cold box on the butcher's wagon, the solar fresnel welder . . . *that* scared the heck out of me!" Merridel said.

"Why now??"

Merridel shrugged. "Maybe some traders found a mechanic-minded town. Maybe some town miles from here has revived a steel mill or something."

"You need *old* power for one of those!" Julia picked up and tapped a quill against the side of the writing desk. Merridel hadn't seen her this anxious since their wedding.

"I wish I could tell you why now—but they're showing up, so we have to ask: Do we use them or not?"

"That's the town's decision."

"Of course. But you and the Outreach Guild provide the info for the vote."

"You as librarian, also. Can't you find some fact that will get Thoma off my neck? Dammit—look over there!"

Through the door, Merridel noticed Thoma by the keg in the corner, gesturing with one hand as he lectured nonstop, clearly trying to convince Venkat of something.

"He's sidestepping proper channels!" Julia exclaimed.

"Definitely out of bounds," Merridel muttered. "I'll go tell Venkat that Winter Gardening's back."

She'd barely stepped into the room when the main door opened and Dale, Yellow and a red-haired boy stepped in. Their faces were set in tense frowns and at first Merridel thought there'd been an accident. But Yellow pulled a small notebook from her pocket—Merridel recognized her own work—and in a hog-calling voice announced, "We would like to address the honorable Guild members, their respected guests—"

"What's this all about??" Thoma rushed over, his hand raised to grab Yellow's shoulder.

"As *Mayor*," Julia's voice cut through the surprised babble, "I am minded to hear her out."

Thoma turned in shock, took a deep breath, then pursed his lips. His eyebrows nearly met over his nose; his frown would've won Old Granny status at any fair.

With a panicky glance, Yellow continued, softer now that she had the group's attention. "We respectfully ask the Guild to add two seats, for citizens between the ages of sixteen and nineteen."

"There's a proper meeting for this!" Venkat protested.

"But you won't put us on the agenda," Dale countered. He visibly braced himself.

"And you're making decisions that will affect us more than yourselves!" the redhead added.

And this morning I was worrying about things being too routine, Merridel thought.

"Actually, I believe a discussion like this should come to the General Counsel, where all citizens are represented," Julia said.

"The youth aren't," Yellow retorted, then looked apologetic. Merridel was impressed—she'd thought her scribe was a shallow young thing. But apparently she was interested in town affairs. Maybe *she* had found the info for Dale?

"We'll give you a half-hour at the next meeting, and take it from there, shall we?" Julia said smoothly, walking up to shake their hands. "I appreciate your alerting me to an issue I wasn't aware of."

She escorted them from the room, and immediately the chatter grew loud. Merridel heard " . . . nerve of them!" but also ". . . have a point. It's their future . . ." Guild members apologized profusely to their guests, who looked both disapproving and smug. *Always good to know another town has it worse.*

She suddenly realized Thoma had left. She hurried to the front hall; Julia and Thoma were arguing—obviously Julia was trying to stop him from slapping an infraction on the young folk—breach of peace, or being young without a license. Merridel bit her lip to keep from grinning. It really wasn't funny . . .

"Machines lead to destruction!" Thoma was saying.

"Only if they're used badly," Merridel interjected, walking over. "They're just sophisticated tools."

"No—they do something to the mind," he argued, gesturing furiously. "Once you have a capability beyond human abilities, you cannot help but use it." He faced them. "Did you know they used to take hearts out of bodies and put others in? My grandfather told me."

"Divine spare us! That's impossible! *Why??*" Julia exclaimed.

"It *was* possible then," he told her. "And why? Because they wanted to live forever, and they found out that stealing someone else's heart gave them a few more years. I heard rumors—not that I believe this—but some people were trying to turn themselves into machines, or put themselves in a machine, thinking that they'd never die."

Merridel shook her head—she'd seen some very old magazines, with horrible pictures, but it still seemed impossible. She'd assumed those were the famous horror stories the Oil Culture enjoyed.

"And people walked around with metal hips, knees, or whole legs made of machines," Thoma continued.

"But in any case, Dale had no intention of anything—" Merridel protested.

"It's a slippery slope! The reason we instituted sustainable labor was to avoid being helpless without machines. And now they want to overturn our well-thought -out rules!"

"All we know is that they want to be part of the discussion," Julia said. There were spots of red on her cheeks; Merridel knew she was close to saying something she might regret.

But Thoma was oblivious. "Besides, it disrespects the divine complexity of Gaia," he continued. "In order to have machines you have to have square-cut mind."

"Square-cut . . . ?" Merridel was puzzled.

Thoma gestured impatiently. "In order for machines to work, they had to cut things to the same size; they had to toss and waste anything that didn't fit—and that included humans!"

"But without *some* standardization, things like Morse code wouldn't be available, and surely you don't think that—" With a sinking heart, Merridel realized Thoma *did* think that was too much.

"People should just tell each other—dots and dashes take the life out of the message," Thoma muttered.

"Without telegraph, we'd have no warning of bad weather," Merridel argued. "That storm warning last Fall saved lives, and we got a lot of the oats more securely stowed." Something crystallized in Merridel's thoughts. "Thoma, you're trying to avoid making mistakes."

"Of course I am!" he said scornfully.

"But that's not possible. 'To err on the side of caution' is *still* to err. And Gaia's plan is dynamic —what was right today isn't always right tomorrow. So our rules have to shift as things change."

The door opened and Venkat stuck his head out. "The formal presentation is starting," he said apologetically and ducked back in.

"I need to be there," Julia said. "This discussion will wait." She glared at Thoma, then left.

Merridel faced the Marshal. "I researched today—Dale was correct, and you've abused your power. You should've asked me to check the details."

His face flushed. "You'd have been on her side," he said bitterly.

"Side? Taking sides? You can't keep the peace with such a warlike attitude."

"You've seen the photos of the ruined cities! You of all people, Merridel, have seen the images of destruction. *Why* would you risk another disaster like that?"

No one wanted that, of course, but it was like being terrified of rainstorms because someone had been hit by lightning. And Denio's hiding the reeds was like a child avoiding Mother's eye . . . what had gotten into folks?? Something was seriously skewed. Something Thoma had just said niggled at her—*when you have capacity beyond human abilities you can't help but use it.* That was true of authority as well.

"Thoma, you can't unilaterally change the rules we've set. You have a choice— rescind Dale's punishment or I file a complaint. But perhaps you're correct, and it's time for another Revision."

His face lit up. "Do you . . . mean that? Julia thinks—"

"I'm a citizen; I have my own opinions. It looks like enough has changed that *all* of us need to discuss this, not just a committee." *And there's no guarantee your opinion will win,* she added silently.

"I look forward to your lending your voice to the motion." He paused, then added, "I'll reverse Dale's infraction tomorrow." To her relief, he left by the front door.

Merridel paused with her hand on the chamber door handle. No, she couldn't face the rest of that—she needed quiet and solitude. Julia would understand.

That evening, as they were sitting on the back porch with glasses of berry wine, picking out constellations, Merridel told Julia about the infraction.

"So Dale wasn't at fault at all?" By the flickering oil lamp, she saw the relief and triumph in her partner's face—this was why Julia had wanted her as Witness.

"No—Thoma was overreacting because he's worried about all the new devices. Too much too fast."

"That's why I said we needed the committee," Julia said, then put her hand over her mouth.

"I understand—that's Council business. But like you said tonight, about a bigger forum being needed . . . I think it's time for, well—for a Revision."

Julia almost spilled her wine. "You don't know what you're asking!! It could overthrow everything!"

Merridel patted her hand. "I *do* know what I'm asking—I've read the transcript of the last Revision. But I'm seeing the cracks already—love, you can't hold back change when it's ripe, any more than you can stop a bulb from pushing up through the soil in spring. Like I told Thoma, you can't avoid mistakes, you can only make your best choice and accept the consequences. And who knows? You could go down in history as the wise leader who led us to the next phase of recovery."

Julia was silent for a long time, and Merridel braced herself.

"Well, maybe Thoma has a point," Julia said. "Maybe one of our criteria for judging would be how much waste something created—it's not efficiency if it doesn't use resources well. But if it does, and it saves some labor—"

"Saving labor in one area frees us to do something else that might be just as important. There *must* be a balance between extremes, and if we're careful, we can find it."

"At least we don't have the temptations of the Oil Culture—those days are gone forever."

"And we aren't foolish enough to think that Divine resources are 'free,' and therefore valueless," Merridel said. "And if we stay small enough to know each other, we'll realize that everything comes from *somebody's* labor, and therefore we won't disregard it. I hope."

Julia smiled at Merridel. "That's one thing I love you for—you have a wonderful way of putting things together."

Merridel was surprised. "*You're* the one who's logical and good detail," she protested.

"But you have . . . what did they call it? Intuition. You're good at putting things together differently. I've always been impressed with that."

Putting things together differently? Merridel was amused and pleased. And it certainly looked like this next year would be far more interesting than she'd imagined. Change and stasis, like breathing in and out. A process Gaia had created, that they needed to honor. She savored the wine and watched the ancient, ageless stars, feeling the wind's breath on her cheek.

Don't miss Catherine McGuire's new novel, *Lifeline*, now available in print and e-book formats via Founders House Publishing!

Learn more and purchase a copy for yourself at
http://www.foundershousepublishing.com/2017/03/lifeline-novel.html

REVIEWS

The Spark
by David Drake

Baen Books, 2017

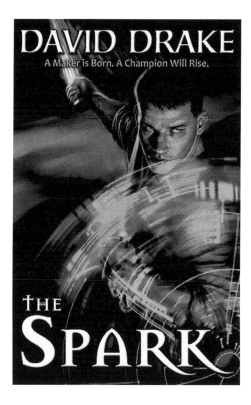

MY READING HAS BEEN ALL OVER the map these days. It's just one of the hazards faced by a public library employee. I like to keep deindustrial science fiction as a staple of my literary diet, but sometimes (every day) I get distracted by the sheer number of titles I come across and have access to. I can tell you, it hasn't necessarily helped with my self-diagnosed, industrial society-induced ADHD. It *has* helped to continue to foster my curiosity and creativity.

As the Christmas holiday encroached upon me, and as 2017 wound down to its last days, I found myself in desperate need of escapist literature to get over my bah humbug blues. Deindustrial SF doesn't exactly fit the escapist bill, as it confronts the possible consequences of humanity's collective actions as they spiral into the future. We and our descendants can't escape those consequences however they may happen to play out. Deindustrial SF does however fit the entertainment bill, all while having plausible and believable futures. I was going to pass on taking home the advance reader copy of *The Spark* by David Drake that I saw at work. I hadn't ever read Drake before. I'd relegated him to the "Military SF" subgenre, which I'd never thought would appeal to me. I changed my mind though when I opened it up and read the author's introduction and was inclined to give it a shot. It had two things going for it: it was set in a distant deindustrial future, and it riffed on Arthurian legends.

In his intro, Drake discussed an idea, the Three Matters, originally proposed by Jean Bodel, who was a twelfth century poet from France. Bodel wrote that there were three main topics for romance storytellers (not the pulp paperback romances with muscle-bound firemen or Scottish lairds on the covers). These matters are the Matter of Rome, the Matter of France, and the

Matter of Britain and were stories based on geographic location and characters from history and legend. Basically Bodel was the first person to classify the main themes of medieval literature into categories. The Matter of Rome retells stories from classical antiquity, the Matter of France is chiefly concerned with Charlemagne and his heroic paladins, and the Matter of Britain is about King Arthur, his knights of the Round Table and related matters.

For *The Spark*, Drake chose to use the Matter of Britain to hang a tale of the distant future on. His novel was based on the Lancelot stories yet he clothed them in a world where the technology of a past civilization still exists but remains cloaked in mystery. Legacy tech can still be used but it is only able to be worked on by certain folks called makers who have a gift for entering into the machines and working on their structure in a way that is psychic or magical. That gift is part nature and part nurture. The hero of this tale is a young man named Pal, both a maker and a warrior in the making. When he leaves his rural home to go to the city of Dun Add to become a Champion he eventually meets a man named Guntram, a sort of a Merlin figure, who becomes his mentor.

Much of the remaining tech that washes into the towns and cities comes from a vast wasteland that exists between inhabited settlements. Monsters also lurk in the waste, making forays into the human world. Some of these creatures used to be men who became deranged and mutated into something else. Other creatures are completely other. Connecting the settlements are passages through the waste, called the Road. Travel on the Road is made dangerous by the monsters from the waste. And the cities and towns have a hard time maintaining unity with each other in a damaged world.

A leader figure has arisen in Dun Add, a parallel of Arthur in Camelot. His goal is to try to reunite the scattered settlements into a cohesive whole. Pal, as the Lancelot figure, stumbles into this world, growing up over the course of the novel, making it something of a *bildungsroman*. He goes from being a country bumpkin ill at ease with city life to a capable man of the world, and a strong fighter, along the way.

I liked the action, adventure and bravado of this book enough that I'm going to read some more of Drake's stories. From what I've learned he uses historical personages and scenarios quite often in his other books. I'll especially be keen for a sequel to *The Spark*. Maybe I'll look to Drake again next December for help in getting through the holiday season intact.

This book has also gotten me interested in the work of some related writers, who work in the Military SF and Alternate History subgenres: guys like S. M. Stirling, Eric Flint and John Ringo. They all seem to have a lot of fun playing with history and repurposing it in various ways. I've started reading Stirling's *Emberverse* series and one of the things that struck me was his deliberate use of alien space bats (a.k.a. deus ex machina events) that change the course of history in one fell swoop. While that is a literary device deindustrial SF seeks to sidestep, there are some interesting things to be gleaned from reading these guys, with their knowledge of history at the forefront. I think the Three Matters, alongside some other geography, legends and histories that also matter (the Matter of Egypt, the Matter of Japan, the Matter of Scandanavia . . .) would be useful waters to fish from for fellow deindustrial SF writers who are looking to pull up a big one from the deep. (Minus the alien space bats.) Here is to happy fishing and a toast to Clio, the muse of history, who provides inspiration from the past and for the future histories yet to be written.

— *Justin Patrick Moore*
sothismedias.com

Keep Up to Date on Into the Ruins!

Follow our blog for updates on the newest issues, special sales, editorials you won't find in the magazine, and other great content.

Visit us at

intotheruins.com/blog

Year Two has come to an end!
Don't miss a single issue of Into the Ruins

Already a subscriber? Your subscription may be expiring now that Year Two has come to an end!

Renew Today

Visit intotheruins.com/renew
or send a check for $39 made out to Figuration Press to the address below

Don't forget to include the name and address attached to your current subscription and to note that your check is for a renewal. Your subscription will be extended for four more issues.

Subscribe Today

Visit intotheruins.com/subscribe
or send a check made out to Figuration Press for $39 to:

Figuration Press
3515 SE Clinton Street
Portland, OR 97202

Don't forget to include your name and mailing address, as well as which issue you would like to start with.

Made in the USA
Columbia, SC
10 March 2018